The night was like a wild vision taken directly from many of Hilary's past fantasies. The erotic dance of her mistress, the silky cord winding around her body; Oliver tearing the fulfillment away from her, forcing the drama in another direction. It was a scene far removed from the quiet sensuality of Hilary's first encounter with them, the day that she had sealed her fate to become part of this drama.

Hilary realized that she had entered a world where she had no control, and this realization gave her indescribable pleasure.

THE APPLICANT

Lizbeth Dusseau

MASQUERADE BOOKS, INC.
801 SECOND AVENUE
NEW YORK, N.Y. 10017

The Applicant

Copyright © 1992 by Lizbeth Dusseau
All Rights Reserved

No part of this book may be reproduced, stored in a retrieval system, or transmitted in any form, by any means, including mechanical, electronic, photocopying, recording or otherwise, without prior written permission of the publishers.

First Masquerade Edition 1992

Third Printing February 1997

ISBN 1-56333-501-8

First Top Shelf Edition 1997
ISBN 1-56333-895-5

Manufactured in the United States of America
Published by Masquerade Books, Inc.
801 Second Avenue
New York, N.Y. 10017

CHAPTER I

One

ADVENTURESOME YOUNG WOMAN WHO ENJOYS BEING SUBMISSIVE SOUGHT BY MARRIED COUPLE IN EARLY FORTIES. LONG-TERM RELATIONSHIP DESIRED. EXPECT NO LIMITS.

"Good afternoon," she said, looking the young woman up and down appreciatively. "You must be Hilary."

"Yes. Good afternoon," the younger woman answered.

Liza relished the sight of the exquisite young woman before her. Her features were elegant, with beautifully sculptured cheekbones, brown eyes that held some innocence, but turned up at the corners suggestively, and lips that were perfect—full with a deep natural red blush that combined alluringly with her dark olive skin. The young woman's hair was waist length and shone in the morning sun; her hair was created to be touched, Liza thought. She was a natural beauty and needed few cosmetics to bring out what had been given her in the way of bodily grace and charm.

Liza could detect the swell of the younger woman's breasts as she stood rather cautiously before her. Her waist was small, which accentuated her graceful hips and the shape of her tits. Her ass was well framed in the short, tight skirt she wore. Everything about her enticed Liza. She was *the one*.

"Sit down, Hilary." She directed Hilary through the living room to a comfortable chaise longue covered in soft velvet. The sun streamed through the French windows of the morning room, the muted light playing tricks of illusion in the younger woman's exquisite hair and deep brown eyes. Hilary was clearly unique among Liza's applicants, and she had seen many young women since she had placed the advertisement in the classifieds two weeks earlier. Liza could sense a desire taking shape between the two of them already, as though the sexual energy actually manifested itself as matter between them in the lazy heat of the morning sun. It was a desire that was born of both their needs.

"Hilary, may I ask you why you chose to answer the advertisement?"

"It spoke of submission," the younger woman responded shyly.

Yet Liza could tell by the way the young woman carried herself she was not shy, perhaps just overwhelmed by her own desire to answer such an advertisement. She could tell that Hilary was inexperienced, and the thought made her all the more enticing.

The Applicant

"It is something that I have wanted for a long time," said Hilary, looking down at a spot of sunlight on the Spanish tile floor of the morning room.

Liza smiled inwardly, for she could well understand the desire.

"Have you ever been submissive to anyone else?"

"Yes. I had a lover who enjoyed dominating me, but as my needs became more complicated, he could no longer satisfy me," she replied, looking up from the tile to meet Liza's unmoving gaze.

The two women stared at one another for a long moment. Hilary was perfect, thought Liza, especially the way she kept her head held regally while keeping her eyes downcast—a perfect submissive.

Liza's desire for this young woman before her was growing rapidly, for Hilary had a sensual quality that exuded from her being; it was a sexuality that ran deeper than the obvious appeal of her youthful body.

"You understand, Hilary, that my husband Oliver and I seek mutual satisfaction. If you decide to be trained by us, we will concentrate on understanding your desires as well as on fulfilling our own. Is that understood?"

"Yes," Hilary said. Her voice was smooth and velvety, sultry, yet innocent.

Liza was so attracted to the young woman that she was gripped by the desire to plunge her fingers into Hilary's silky hair and to explore the length of her body. Her hands would make the way downward until they could tease the lips of the cunt that hid beneath the tight fabric of Hilary's silk skirt. But Liza's pleasure would have to be put off, for there were steps that must be taken to establish the implicit trust that was absolutely necessary between a submissive and master or mistress. There would be time, thought Liza, there would be time enough for all that and more.

"If you decide to embark on this sensual adventure with us, you must be ready to confront the darker side of sexual pleasure." Liza paused and looked at Hilary for a long time, reading the young woman's excitement and fear. She paused a moment more to let the unknown take hold of Hilary's imagination for a moment.

"There will be great intensity that can only be bearable if one has made a great commitment to pleasure. We will expect a great deal from you if you choose to make this commitment to the relationship. The pleasure you experience will not be without the light of sexuality; for we cannot have the dark without the light, no?" Liza raised her eyebrows at Hilary inquisitively.

"I understand," was all Hilary said.

Hilary had looked directly at Liza as she answered, and Liza appreciated the simplicity of her response. There was a certain animal quality, a certain kind of sensual focus about Hilary that would serve her and Oliver very well indeed. Of course, Oliver would notice Hilary's unusual sexual aura immediately.

"You understand that it will be required that you perform intelligently, aggressively. Can you be aggressive?"

"Yes," Hilary answered.

Liza was convinced that she would receive anything she asked of the younger woman.

Hilary in her own turn was magnetically drawn to Liza. The woman had a sense of authority that Hilary had been longing for in a female lover. She was attracted to Liza's grace and maturity, which posed a vague and exciting threat to Hilary's inexperience.

The Applicant

She sensed that Liza was a woman from whom she could learn many things, a woman who could give her the training she needed and desired.

Hilary was taken with the surroundings of the estate immediately, and as she chanced to look about the morning room, she felt that the place held her as firmly in its seduction as did the woman lounging before her. The sun filtered in through the windows, making the air dance with dust and pollen. Everything in the room was sensual, and the warmth of the day gave her the sensation that everything about her was floating in the raw sensuality of their words.

She had been so hesitant to answer the advertisement, so fearful that she would find herself in the company of a dark, self-centered mistress whose arrogance and lack of subtlety she would be unable to abide. Yet now as she looked at Liza, it seemed that she had found what she desired, more than she hoped to articulate even in her fantasies. She still had some lingering doubts about diving into this specialized and secret world of sexuality; she wondered if she could make the commitment, and keep it, now that she knew what Liza would demand of her.

"I can sense your hesitation," Liza said, breaking into Hilary's thoughts. "But I believe you want to stay." She spoke with a command that was somehow laced with gentleness, and her words soothed Hilary.

"I *am* nervous," Hilary replied. "To be perfectly frank, I am fascinated by you, and that frightens me."

"It is natural to be afraid of the unknown, but you must keep in mind that what Oliver and I offer is the opportunity for you to live the way you most desire, to experience the sheer sexual abandon you long for. You will be giving yourself a rare gift that few risk giving into."

The telephone rang in another part of the house and Liza excused herself to answer it. As she left the room, Hilary watched her move with great appreciation. Liza's body was catlike and youthful; her long legs and every curve of her body were accentuated by the skintight black leggings she wore. Her white silk shirt billowed over them; it was so diaphanous that Hilary could easily see the shape and form of Liza's breasts and nipples beneath the thin fabric. Her breasts were not large, but were round and perfectly formed; her nipples were large and dark, and Hilary could not help noticing that they had stood erect during the interview. Hilary was enticed by Liza's soft red hair and the way it framed her face in loose curls, hanging about her shoulders and back. That fiery hair set off her exquisite eyes—hazel eyes that seemed to shift in hue as the light in the room changed. Those eyes had held Hilary in thrall. She was so taken by Liza, she could feel the depth of her longing begin to well between her legs. She walked out into the hallway and located a bathroom; she found her panties were wet and her pussy was juicy.

When she returned, Hilary took the opportunity to walk around the room, examining it more closely. It seemed to her that Liza was made for the morning room, or was the morning room made for her? The beautiful, light-filled room was part of a sensual house that was well kept and seemed to somehow belie the secrets hidden in its walls—in its history. The house seemed to Hilary a perfect surrounding for sensual play, and she was almost as attracted to it as she was to its mistress. It seemed to give off the perfume of decadence from another era. It was surrounded by lawns of green and dozens of beds of red roses that were simultane-

The Applicant

ously beautiful and ominous, like the house. Like Liza.

"I'm sorry to keep you waiting, Hilary," Liza said as she returned to the room.

"Not at all. I've been enjoying the room. It is lovely."

"Thank you, I love it too. I love the whole place. It is a house with many features that vary greatly from this room. Rooms that would give you an altogether different perspective of the house. Sometimes I think I could stay here without ever leaving."

Liza sank back into her soft velvet chaise longue and motioned to a small settee where Hilary was to sit. She gazed at her prospective lover with a kind of detached curiosity. She seemed to be planning her next words very carefully. Her voice changed rather suddenly as her demeanor assumed a colder distance.

"Take off your blouse and let me see your breasts," she said to Hilary.

Hilary hesitated only a moment, and instantly regretted her hesitation; she began to slowly unbutton the tiny pearl buttons of her soft cotton shirt. She felt her loins ache as her body acknowledged her desire.

"Remove it all the way," said Liza.

The blouse fell away from Hilary's shoulders, and Liza gazed at the breasts barely encased in an elegant white bra, the cups of which were cut brief so that Hilary's nipples were nearly visible. Hilary cast her eyes down, fearful that her face would betray too much emotion. The sexual tension between herself and Liza was like nothing she had ever experienced before. In times past when she had intimately exposed herself to a new lover, the moment seemed to be diminished by his masculine need to dive into her flesh. Liza simply appreciated her body as Hilary sat before her. In doing so, Hilary realized that Liza was creating an exquisite moment, allowing the two of them to relish the excitement and intimacy in the revealing of one's nudity.

"Look at me," said Liza with authority, but not without affection.

Hilary looked into Liza's wonderful eyes. She let her gaze wander over Liza's sensuous lips and soft pale skin.

"You are a most desirable creature, Hilary. Come here. On your knees. Come here, close to me," she commanded. Hilary slid slowly off the settee and moved forward so that she sat on a soft rug in front of Liza.

Liza paused, and then leaned forward and moved her finger lightly over Hilary's flesh. The pale complexion of her own skin contrasted lightly with Hilary's rich olive-toned flesh. Liza reached around behind Hilary's back and deftly unhooked the bra, allowing it to fall to the floor. Hilary's breasts were full and firm, and her nipples small and hard, sitting high, like two delectable cherries on the young woman. Liza ran her fingers very lightly over the enticing nipples, barely touching Hilary, and then suddenly she began to pinch one, and then the other, rather hard, watching the sensations shower Hilary's body. It was as though her flesh were a conduit of electricity, her skin so soft to the touch, so fragrant, with a light sheen of sweat covering her skin, making her glow in the sunlight. Liza felt the familiar lurch of desire between her legs and on the tips of her own nipples, which grew hard as she caressed Hilary's.

Hilary rocked softly with the alternating gentle, then painful caress of Liza's hands. She felt faint with a rush of pleasure, and she seemed to be suspended in sensual heat for several moments. She could hear her own throat making low noises, and her breath was becoming louder and irregular.

The Applicant

"Unfasten your skirt," Liza said, in a voice accustomed to knowing control, even in highly charged situations.

Hilary obediently reached around and unfastened her skirt. She stood to let the fabric fall to the floor, and Liza looked appreciatively at Hilary's firm belly and the smooth swell of her hips. She wore tiny white bikini panties that hid a neatly trimmed dark bush.

"Are you wet?'

"Yes," answered Hilary breathlessly.

"Put your fingers to your cunt and let me see your juice."

Hilary put her hand to her throbbing pussy and found its lips wet with juice. She let her fingers linger there a moment, and then slowly withdrew them.

"Lick them."

Hilary brought her fingers to her mouth and began to tongue them lightly, never taking her eyes from Liza. Hilary's cunt was on fire, and she wanted to cry out and beg for more, but she dared not to reveal all her passion.

"Turn around and let me see your ass," Liza instructed after a few moments.

Hilary turned to show Liza her backside. Liza reached out and lowered Hilary's panties to reveal the young woman's firm buttocks. She noticed that there were no tan lines and was pleased. She slowly ran her hand over the warm, inviting flesh, allowing her fingers to drag along the slightly parted crevice.

"Go to the table by the window," Liza ordered. "In the top drawer you will find a paddle. Bring it to me."

Hilary turned and, before she went to the desk, removed her panties. She strode across the room naked and retrieved a short paddle from the drawer. The paddle had a sturdy handle, with a firm but flexible leather end that had seemingly been well oiled. As she held the instrument, Hilary felt an uncontrolled rush of excitement as she thought of the paddle striking her ass—as she thought of the paddle in Liza's hands.

"Sit down on the stool." Liza motioned to a footstool in front of her. "I want you to look at your instrument carefully. Feel it. Smell it. Smell the leather if you like."

Hilary fingered the paddle with deliberation, and as she felt the weight of the instrument in her hand, the urges within her grew. She wanted to stroke it all over her body. She wanted Liza to stroke it all over her body, a prelude to what she hoped would be more forceful strokes.

"You'd like to feel the touch of it on your sweet little ass, wouldn't you?"

Hilary nodded.

"And I'd like nothing better myself than to give you a good paddling." She paused and smiled wickedly. "Ah, but that will have to wait. Nothing may progress in this arrangement until we are both certain that this is what we want. Do you understand?"

"Yes."

Hilary trembled at the sound of Liza's words. Her fear and desire were competing for dominance within her own body.

"You will need to stay here for three or four weekends, after which you will return to your regular life. When that time is over and your training is complete, we will discuss how we'd like our relationship to continue," she paused, "if we want our relationship to continue."

As she spoke, Hilary watched her seductive lips and wished for nothing more than to kiss them, bite

The Applicant

them, to entwine her tongue with Liza's. Her desire was so intense, she felt as though she were entering a new reality.

"You must consider this proposal carefully. Of course you are free to quit your training at any time. But it is essential that you do not decide too quickly. Sometimes hasty decisions turn out to be the wrong ones.

"I'd like you to return next Friday. If you wish to stay, bring your clothing for the weekend. Call me if you decide not to come. Please do not make any final decisions until Friday."

As Liza spoke, Hilary continued to caress the paddle lovingly, enjoying the lovely form.

"There is nothing that I've wanted more," replied Hilary with longing. How she longed to feel the bitter pleasure of the paddle against her flesh; how she longed to feel Liza closer to her, dominating her, touching her.

"I understand, but now is not the time," said Liza, maintaining exquisite control even though she wanted to reach out and take Hilary immediately.

Hilary was thoroughly seduced. Her whole body felt the need for satisfaction and she felt it was a cruel punishment that Liza ordered, not to proceed that very day with her first session. Yet Hilary instinctively knew it was a wise order, realizing that it was clothed in the rare kind of consideration and care that she wanted.

"Get dressed," said Liza finally. "And return the paddle to the drawer; that is where it will always be found."

Liza watched her as she re-dressed with a little tinge of regret, but she quickly collected herself and proceeded to show Hilary around the house. Beyond the morning room there was a breakfast room and large kitchen. Each of these spaces were bright and airy, rooms filled with flowers and light and all the sensuous warmth that Hilary felt Liza exuded simultaneously within her role as dominant mistress.

Liza led her outside from the kitchen, down a stairway, and along a rose-lined path that led to a terrace. The terrace and the pool beyond were set with a different pattern of lovely hand-painted Spanish tiles, and around the pool grew African daisies and sunflowers. Old-fashioned wood and wicker furniture surrounded the pool, giving the whole scene a feeling of decadence and style from days long gone.

Liza turned to Hilary and said cryptically, "There are other buildings to be explored at a later time; perhaps when you return. I think you'll find some of their secrets most exciting."

One building appeared to be a small barn that might have been a stable at one time. Another similar structure was further down the lawn, and it appeared to have an apartment in the second story.

Hilary followed Liza up a flight of stairs once they were back inside the house. Soon they found themselves in a formal dining room. The room was simple and comfortable and betrayed the fact that Liza and her husband had a great deal of money. But the room was remarkably different to Hilary in that it didn't have the warmth of the other rooms of the house. The living room across the hall held the same feeling for her. It was a masculine feeling, and the sensation was more detached and remote than the rooms that seemed to be extensions of Liza's personality. Clearly these rooms were the extension of Oliver's personality. Oliver. The word and the thought of him sent new chills of excitement through her body; Hilary wondered when she would meet him.

As Liza and Hilary at last stood at the front door,

The Applicant

Liza said, "Consider your decision well. It may have rather startling consequences for you."

It seemed to Hilary for a moment that Liza might reach out to her, take her face in her hands and kiss her, but her hopes were not realized. Instead, Hilary smiled her good-bye, her eyes lowered submissively.

Liza watched from the front porch as the woman drove down the long drive to the road.

Inside again, she picked up the hall phone and dialed a single number.

"Oliver," she said, "she is lovely."

"Yes, I saw her."

"I'll be up later." There was an aching desire in her voice, and an ache in her body that needed to be satisfied.

He said nothing, and Liza smiled.

CHAPTER II

Two

For the second time, Hilary climbed the steps to the sprawling frame house on the lake, ready to explore the secretive adventures that had been alluded to on her previous visit. It had been a long week of waiting. She really didn't feel it was necessary to wait as long to make a decision as Liza had forced her to do, for Hilary knew her answer immediately, and her thoughts had not wavered since the moment she drove away from the house and away from Liza. Of course Liza had known the answer as well, but it was essential that they play out this erotic waiting game, this erotic drama of anticipation and a certain threatening fear of the unknown.

Hilary's decision haunted her each day as she went to work at the bank. She would sit behind her teller's window, dressed rather primly, knowing, fantasizing, dreaming of the rare opportunity that she had elected to take advantage of. Her considerations and thoughts made her feel imminently different, and these internal changes became more apparent as her co-worker Andrew peered over her shoulder as she worked. Ordinarily she found his presence exciting, and they had slept together more than once, but today she found his closeness almost annoying and invasive.

"How about Friday night?" he whispered to her.

"I'm busy," she replied, concentrating on her work in order to dissuade him from questioning her further.

"Saturday?"

"No," she said.

"You trying to tell me something?" he asked, gently brushing his hand discreetly over her thigh.

"Stop it," she hissed. She was no longer interested in his touch.

There was a time when Andrew's lips on her cunt were ... acceptable. But his pussy-eating techniques and overall sexuality were never really enough for Hilary.

He was a nice enough guy—and maybe that was the problem—but he was just too drab. With Liza, Hilary had been turned on to a possibility that made her pussy tingle.

Andrew had fucked her well, the times they did get together; and she recalled the warm feeling she got when he drove his nice, thick cock into her wet, waiting opening. But he was always so ... predictable.

With a man like Andrew, Hilary always knew what would happen. He'd start with her tits, fondling them from outside her shirt, finally undoing her bra. He'd grab them and squeeze them and take the taut nip-

The Applicant

ples in his mouth and suck, beginning to moan in a way his parents would never have dreamt their baby boy could talk. Then he'd take her hand and put it on his hard cock, just so she could feel what she was doing to him: With his other hand he'd coax her head down, onto the swollen tool.

"Suck it," he'd say. "Suck me, baby."

He'd pull her head down on his dick and would moan. She'd suck him so good that his come would be just at the edge. And then he'd want to fuck. He'd want to get inside that warm, tight hole as fast as he could, because his dick was about to boil over and he wanted to let it go—just like that!

There was no control, no deep passion, no eroticism with a guy like Andrew. There was just dinner, maybe a show, and then, if he was lucky, a fuck. He didn't eat pussy as a policy, so when he did do it, it was sweet. And Hilary didn't mind opening herself to the tongue and letting him lash her up and down, in and out. But he never made her come; and he always came too quickly.

When Andrew went home, Hilary would have to really fuck herself—just to relieve her sexual tension. She usually used her fingers and usually came by rubbing her clit really hard. In her dreams, there was a secret lover who would lick her come-drenched fingers, and then spank her for fucking herself without his permission. In her fantasies, there were no men like Andrew. There were only men with big cocks who liked to tie her up before fucking; and women, with eager mouths who could eat pussy and spank at the same time. Women who were not afraid to go tongue to tongue with another woman—women like Liza who exuded sexuality, who made you want them.

She wanted Liza's touch, her hands, her intensity

and warmth. And Oliver, too. Hilary knew she desired him, even without knowing him. It was his presence that she'd felt in the house, and the thought of him now—the mysterious vibration of his being in the rooms of the house—made her shiver involuntarily. She was ready to confront the side of herself that desired to be part of a seductive world where there were no boundaries, no limitations. A world far away from the banality of her work at the bank, away from the conventional evenings in her bedroom.

Everything she did that week was colored by the possibilities of what might transpire that next weekend. When she woke in the middle of Tuesday night, her body on fire, sweating with desire, her hands involuntarily found themselves between her legs, stroking her hot pussy. Her fingers worked the lips of her cunt as her other hand stroked and pinched her own breast. She felt so guilty, touching the body that was to be Liza's; she felt she was cheating on her mistress. But her boiling pussy would not be denied, or ignored. She took herself to orgasm over and over again, continuing to masturbate through the long night, and even until the sun came creeping into her room early the next morning.

The velocity of her thoughts kept her from rising in time for work that morning. In her imagination she saw the paddle in her hands and wanted nothing more than to feel it against her flesh. She wanted to be taken deep into the world of sexuality that had consumed her thoughts and fantasies for years—desires of complete submission, of laying her body out for others to use, of losing herself in sex for days on end ... desires for other women and their soft, sure hands. She had been swimming all week in a sea of dreams that were about to materialize in her reality, and the possibility of these desires becoming

The Applicant

manifest in her life filled her with a delicious kind of fear—a kind of fear that she could smell, a fear she could taste.

And now she found herself climbing the steps of the mysterious old house that sat out in the country, remote and beautiful in its seclusion. Hilary reached out and rang the doorbell.

"Liza's at the pool. I'll show you there," said the maid who answered the door.

As she walked down the mahogany-paneled entry, Hilary felt at once embraced by the faint familiarity of the house. Her senses were filled with the smell of the fresh-cut flowers that filled vases in each room, of the well-oiled wood and the soft leather. She followed the robust maid through the hallway that led into the morning room, and then down the stairs to the terrace and out to the pool. The maid left her at the doorway after pointing to where Liza was reclining nude in the sun.

Hilary drew in her breath at the beauty of Liza's perfect body, still slightly damp from a recent swim and dappled by the afternoon sun. She also noticed that Liza was not alone. A man with deeply tanned skin was stroking Liza's naked body with slow, passionate deliberation. His hands ran languourously up and down Liza's thighs and now and again his fingers dipped into the nakedness of her cunt which Hilary was surprised to find shaved perfectly bare. Hilary watched, barely breathing, as his hands began to stroke Liza's breasts, his fingers toying with her nipples and then slapping the tender flesh. Then his face disappeared between the soft mounds; yet Hilary could still see his mouth from time to time cover the enlarged nipples as he licked and bit them.

The thrill of watching their lovemaking sent deep pangs of pleasure through Hilary's body, and she wanted to be with them, she wanted to be touched by them. She especially wanted to be touched by Liza, and felt even a little jealously possessive of the beautiful woman. She watched silently as the man entered Liza, and Hilary drew in her breath, experiencing the sensation vicariously. The young man's tanned flesh was a perfect compliment to Liza's milky white skin. He was over her, smiling, as her eyes closed halfway and a grimace of pleasure crossed her lips. Liza's head arched back, and her hips lifted to meet his powerful thrusts. He plunged his cock deeper and deeper still into Liza's cunt, and then slowly withdrew, so that Hilary could see his shaft gleaming in its power, shining with love juice from Liza's cunt. Liza began to buck underneath him, writhing with a passion that Hilary had only dreamed of. She was moaning, and her sounds began to turn into screams of pleasure, screams of orgasm.

He pinned her underneath him, driving into her with his cock, binding her arms over her head with his own hands. Hilary watched, her entire body aflame, as Liza's flesh met with his, her legs wrapping around the small of his back, while she cried out with animal pleasure. Hilary watched his ass muscles contract, as he made one more fierce lunge inside Liza, emitting an animal cry of his own—a sound that came from some bestial place within him. He was coming inside her, and his final thrusts were met with her own, as she milked him with her own orgasm. It seemed to Hilary that the muscles of Liza's pussy were literally pulling him deeper within her, pulling his orgasm out of him.

Hilary could feel the juice of her own excitement as she watched the two collapse into each other in sexual aftermath, their bodies entwined in soft caresses and smiles and confidential laughter. As

The Applicant

Hilary watched, her own lust diminished slightly, for she felt embarrassed at witnessing this intimacy. But her envy did not seem to fade. She wanted to be the one entwined with Liza. Somehow Hilary knew that this beautiful specimen of a male was not Oliver, and she was curious and not a little jealous over Liza's attentions to him. Their sweating bodies held her spellbound, and her mind filled with wonder that such animal pleasure and excitement could really exist. Hilary had never known such sexual freedom with another. She had known pleasure, but her appetite never seemed sated. She found that the passion never lasted with her previous lovers. It seemed that so many of her lovers had been only interested in pleasing themselves and did not take the time or care to know what really pleased her. But that was why Hilary had answered the advertisement. Her quest for satisfaction had brought her to this place, standing here watching this man and woman in a lovely postcoital repose....

"Hilary."

Liza's voice woke her from her daydreams.

"Yes," Hilary answered automatically and approached the lounge where the young man and Liza lay in one another's arms.

"Stephen, meet Hilary."

"Hello," he said, as his body, his sensual voice, and his eyes captured every inch of Hilary's attention.

"Hello," she said, not knowing whether to extend her hand in greeting.

"Hilary is going to spend a few weekends with us, is that right my dear?" said Liza, looking at Hilary.

"Yes."

"Wonderful," replied Liza, obviously delighted with the young woman's decision.

"You will get to know Stephen very well. Very

well indeed. I guess you saw just how delightful that can be."

"Yes," Hilary blushed.

She watched as Stephen stood and pulled on his jeans, slowly drawing the fabric over his ass, thus sadly hiding his well-muscled thighs and his delicious cock and balls.

"I suppose I should be getting back to work. It looks as if you have yours cut out for you this afternoon," he said to Liza, as he glanced knowingly at Hilary.

"That I do." Liza's eyes were filled with playful deviousness. "But Stephen, I'd like you to be present for our first little game. After all, you will be involved in Hilary's training. You'll enjoy its beginning."

"Do I get to take part?" he asked.

"No, you just get to watch."

They both had devilish expressions that passed between them like a secret. For Hilary the anticipation was almost unbearable.

Liza turned to her. "I think we need to get the preliminaries over with." She paused for a moment, and then her demeanor changed.

"Take off your clothes," said Liza. It was an order.

The directness and immediacy of the change that came over Liza's countenance surprised Hilary. The tables had been turned, for as Liza had been bantering with Stephen, she had pulled a light T-shirt over her head, and now both of them were clothed and Liza was asking Hilary to stand naked before them. Obviously, Liza and Stephen had been unembarrassed by their passionate lovemaking on the terrace, yet Hilary felt the blatant humility that her undressing would bring as she stood before these two commanding people.

The Applicant

"Does she need some help?" Stephen asked, with a hint of sarcastic bemusement. Two sets of eyes lazily perused Hilary's body as they waited for her to obey the command.

"I don't think so," Liza replied. "Hilary is quite compliant, just a bit new to this kind of request." Liza turned to Hilary. "My dear?"

Hilary began to unbutton her blouse and pull it loose from her short skirt. As she pulled the shirt away from her body, she revealed her breasts, which nearly spilled out over her small white brassiere. She felt electrical shocks ripple through her body as she let the blouse fall to the tile of the terrace. Hilary felt that undressing in front of these strangers was even more provocative now than it had been only a week before. She felt like the center of attention, as she unsnapped her bra and exposed her erect nipples to the balmy air. She felt her nerve endings straining under the flesh of her skin as her nipples grew tight with the pleasure of being looked at, the pleasure of being admired.

Stephen's eyes did not alter in their gaze as he reclined against a table. He watched Hilary as the sun illuminated her breasts and the tight flesh of her belly, the shadows of light and dark on her skin making her breasts all the more seductive.

"Pinch your nipples," Stephen ordered. His voice was cold and calculated, the command without the intrinsic warmth of Liza's voice.

Hilary complied, cupping her breasts in either hand, her skin tingling with her own touch. She took each nipple between her thumb and index fingers and gave it a deliberate pinch.

"You can do it harder than that," he said, commanding her to continue.

Liza laughed. "I can see you are ready for Act III and we are still in Scene I," she said to Stephen.

"And this is what you've trained me for?" he bantered back.

She smiled at him, her eyes seducing him, her laugh coy and impish.

"Hilary," she turned back to the girl, "do you remember where the paddle is?"

"Yes ma'am."

"Please get it for me."

"Yes, of course," Hilary said, a tingle of excitement shooting down through her pussy as she recalled the feel of the instrument.

Liza and Stephen watched her firm body move lightly toward the house and through the garden door. They were silent in their appreciation.

Hilary returned minutes later with the instrument in hand.

Liza saw the sweat beading in a sheen on Hilary's upper body, and the way her muscles were tensed with anticipation and excitement.

"This is what you want, isn't it?" Liza asked. Her tone was soft, yet not without discipline. The cadence of her voice reminded Hilary of their first meeting. Liza's softness was so accurately timed, especially after her cold demeanor only moments ago, and the affection in her voice reassured Hilary that her training would be sensitive and pleasing.

"Yes it is," Hilary said. She did not gaze down submissively, but answered Liza directly. There was an intuitive rightness about her bold gaze, and Liza clearly appreciated it.

"If it is really what you want, tell me how many strokes you want."

"I—I don't know," stammered Hilary, the question taking her off guard.

"I'd like to see her bent over, taking it long and

The Applicant

hard," Stephen said, his cold aloofness clashing with Liza's assured calm.

"Yes, and you'd like to do it yourself, wouldn't you?" Liza laughed. "You'll get your chance soon enough; now be quiet. This is between Hilary and me." She paused. "Twelve. I think a dozen strokes will be right," Liza said decisively. "Hand me the paddle."

The younger woman obliged.

"Remove your skirt."

Hilary breathed deeply and followed Liza's orders. She lowered the skirt quickly to reveal to her mistress her handsome thighs, her lovely belly, her glistening mound, and her tight buttocks behind. She had consciously not worn any panties, so that when her skirt fell to the tile she stood completely naked in front of Stephen and Liza.

"He'll want her ass, you know," Stephen said.

"Yes, I know," Liza returned, not facing Stephen but staring at Hilary's nudity with a lusty gaze.

Hilary knew that Stephen was referring to Oliver, and she was filled with the exhilarating possibilities of the unknown.

"Come here and bend over," ordered Liza severely.

Hilary instantly stepped forward and bent over her seated mistress, as she followed the order.

Hilary's round ass was exposed to any pleasurable torment that her mistress might mete out. Liza wasted no time in raising her arm and bringing the paddle down on Hilary's bare ass. Liza was slow and harsh with the first six blows, allowing the full sensation of the blows to ripple throughout Hilary's body. And for the last six, Liza gave the flexible paddle a wide stroke, allowing it to smack with greater force on Hilary's reddening flesh. Hilary squirmed with each jolt, her body heat pouring onto Liza's body beneath her.

"Oh, please," Hilary cried out when the number of blows was nearly at its end. The pain she was experiencing was real, and there was a part of her that feared it; yet there was another voice that rose in her mind and tingled through her cunt. It said: "More, give me more." Liza finished at last, making sure that she brought the last blow atop the reddest part of Hilary's ass with a deliberate firmness that was not meant to be forgotten quickly.

Hilary was breathing hard as she lay stretched across Liza's lap recuperating for a moment. She was gulping for air, and tears were stinging her eyes, but she really did not care. She was taking too much pleasure in the feeling of Liza's soft flesh against her own. She wanted whatever her alluring mistress had to offer.

"Stand up."

Hilary rose to face Stephen and Liza. There was a remarkable tension among the three, all desiring the same thing, all wishing to devour each other in sexual hunger. But there was a kind of distinct caution in the air, because it was clear that Stephen and Hilary were not given the permission to act out their desire yet. Liza was in control, and it was for her to say when and how the other two would be allowed to direct their passions. Everything that Liza was doing was maximizing the moment, maximizing every act, every desire.

"That is your first taste of pleasure, my dear," Liza said at last.

"It leaves me hungry for more," Hilary replied. She could still feel the stinging stripes marking the sensitive flesh of her ass.

"She'll have to tolerate a good deal more if she plans to enjoy herself here," Stephen said dispassionately.

The Applicant

"She knows that, don't you my dear?"

"Yes." The warmth on her bottom gave her the most thrilling rush. Despite the pain, the sensation excited her as she knew it would. Hilary wanted more, and this made her a little afraid.

"Good. I'm glad you understand. Our first session is over. Stephen, you can go back to your work. And Hilary, why don't you take a swim. It will soothe you. You can see your room a bit later."

Liza got up and briskly left the poolside, content to leave her charges to follow her orders. Stephen stole one last longing look at Hilary's young, delicious body and then abruptly turned on his heels and left too. As Hilary stood there alone, a host of thoughts and feelings flooded through her body, her flesh tingling with the highly charged emotions. She needed release, she needed more, and she anxiously wondered when that would come.

Her release did not come that afternoon, or even that night. Hilary and Liza dined on the terrace eating cold shrimp, hard cooked eggs, and vegetables on little squares of toast. After the light meal, Liza dismissed her to her room although it was only seven o'clock.

The room was small, located at the end of a long hallway. There was a simple bed, with a pale coverlet of blue, a dresser, and a small closet. The adjoining bath was nearly as large as the bedroom itself and connected to another room through a door, but the door was locked on the other side.

Hilary ran a bath, and removing her clothes, sank into the large tub. The water was luscious and bubbly, the steam laced with the perfume of fragrant oils. She let the heat of the water and the lovely smell encompass her body up to her throat. The bath seemed a perfect end to a divine day, a day rich with new experiences, rich in the sensual atmosphere of the house, the pool, and Liza's sweet body in close proximity to her own; and now this bath. It didn't seem shocking when she felt soft hands massaging her shoulders, reaching down into the water to massage her breasts, then lingering to toy with her nipples.

"Keep your eyes closed, my dear, and enjoy," Liza said softly, cooing into Hilary's ear.

Hilary could feel herself smiling and her body responding to Liza's firm but sensuous caresses. The older woman's hands were warm and exciting as they moved further down Hilary's body to her belly, massaging it, stroking her flesh. And then they moved seductively between her thighs, and lightly over the softness of her mound. Hilary's body came alive at once.

"I want you to shave your pussy, Hilary. Take this razor and shave your cunt clean. I want it soft and naked like my own." Hilary tingled as she remembered the way Liza's pussy had looked when she found her and Stephen making love on the terrace that afternoon; she had longed then for such an exposed sex. It made Liza's bare cunt seem to cry out to be sucked and licked and eaten by any mouth that found it.

Hilary took the razor in her hand and lifted herself from the water, resting her buttocks on the edge of the tub. Her skin was already soft and ready for the razor's strokes. To her delight, Liza reached over and lightly held the lips of her vagina open, so that Hilary was able to get every last hair. The dangerous feel of the steel against her virgin skin was electrifying. The dangerous touch of Liza's fingers were even more electrifying. Hilary could not remember desiring someone as much as she wanted Liza.

The Applicant

"Open wide, my dear. Be certain that all the hair is removed," said Liza, peering at Hilary's clean sex approvingly.

Hilary continued to shave until her flesh was completely clean. She looked languorously into her mistress' eyes. There was nothing now to hide the folds of her hungry sex from view.

Liza moved forward with a hand bracing Hilary's back; her other hand reached between Hilary's shaking thighs to lightly tease the newly revealed flesh.

"You are delightful," Liza said, her voice low with desire.

Hilary gave in to her pleasure and let her hips grind slightly against Liza's fingers. Her orgasm would have been instantaneous, but she used some control, wanting the desire to build, to let the feelings increase in pleasure to the point when she could hold them back no more. She floated back into Liza's caress, her eyes half-closed. Her mistress' deft fingers found the object of her pleasure, and they were exploring the wonderfully hot love holes that were now so beautifully exposed. As Liza's fingers continued to delve deeper and deeper into Hilary's cunt, both women's passions were more fiercely aroused. And then Liza suddenly moved away.

"Not yet my dear. You must wait." And with that, Liza turned and left the bathroom.

There was nothing that Hilary wanted more than for Liza to take her, to give her orgasm after orgasm. She would wait. She did not want to have pleasure without her mistress there with her.

Just as Hilary had that thought, Liza popped her head back in. "Oh, and from here on, please do not bring yourself to orgasm—that would be cheating on me. You can play with that sweet cunt, but you can't make it explode when I am not present." Liza disappeared again, closing the door behind her. Hilary wandered into the bedroom and collapsed onto the bed. She could only dream of what it would have been like to have had Liza continue her play, and to experience Liza's tongue on her clit, flicking the hard bud back and forth until the orgasm rose and exploded within her. She could only pretend that Liza's hands were there still, exploring the sweet pink meat between her legs. And as she imagined these things, it was as if she could feel Liza's tongue tunneling through her wet cunt and then could feel the other woman's own pussy slapped onto her waiting mouth. Hilary could only fantasize what it would be like to splay open Liza's legs and eat her out. She could only imagine what it might feel like to rest her head on Liza's breasts. She could only dream of lying in bed with her mistress, their shaved pussies rubbing against each other, their titties pressing firmly into one another, nipples erect, their bodies entwined. And in her fantasy, Oliver came in, his big, hard cock looking for a temporary home. With this last vision lingering in her mind, Hilary fell into a deep sleep.

CHAPTER III

Three

It was a sumptuous Saturday afternoon. As the shadows lengthened across the terrace and the pool, the day fell all too quickly into evening. The water in the pool lapped gently against the tile as Hilary floated naked, looking into the sky that was turning a deeper blue. The thick, humid day was steadily turning to a balmy evening, and the spring crickets could be heard in the deep lawn and surrounding woods of the estate.

She was being watched from the house. From the second story, eyes wild with lust gazed hungrily in anticipation. Yet the gaze came from the eyes of one who knew the meaning of control and self-discipline. The eyes watched as, water glimmering on her body, Hilary pulled herself from its soft sensuousness. She dried herself with the thick white towel and then pulled a plain white T-shirt over her head. The shirt somehow emphasized her nakedness more than it did anything to cover her.

What was imperceptible to the eyes that watched Hilary were the thoughts and fantasies that whirled inside her mind. She remembered the lovely morning she had spent with her mistress. Slowly she drifted back into the memory, allowing herself to relive it....

"Kneel," Liza had said.

Hilary dropped to her knees and knelt before her mistress, the tiles of the terrace cold on her bare knees. They were both still wet from their early morning swim. Liza leaned down and kissed Hilary on the lips, letting her tongue linger many moments inside the younger woman's mouth. Hilary trembled at the soft warmth of another woman's mouth against her own.

"Stay still," Liza whispered, as she continued to lick her with slow tiny kisses that began at Hilary's lips and then moved down her neck to her aching breasts.

"Do that to me," ordered Liza. And then she lay back against the chaise and spread her long body out in the early morning sun. Hilary rose and slowly approached the object of her heated desire. She slowly took in the sight of Liza's breasts, her shaved cunt, her legs spread and dangling lazily. She placed a delicate kiss on Liza's lips, and then, almost beyond her ability to control her hunger, she dove upon Liza's neck and breasts, suckling at her nipples furiously. She wanted to devour her mistress, she wanted to consume Liza then and there.

Liza was becoming more and more aroused with each passionate moment, with each hungry kiss from the younger woman. She felt Hilary's warm breath on

The Applicant

her flesh and enjoyed the luxurious sensation of the tongue on her erect nipples.

"Kiss them. Suck them," Liza said breathlessly, pressing Hilary's head down hard over her breast, and Hilary obeyed passionately.

"My belly," Liza moaned, and Hilary continued down the swell of her stomach, making tiny circles and biting kisses with her tongue and teeth. Without encouragement, Hilary found her tongue anxiously between Liza's thighs, ready to take her first taste from her sweet pussy, ready to lap hungrily at her clean-shaven flesh. Hilary wanted to devour her with her fingers and lips and tongue; she wanted to explore every secret fold, every inch of Liza's hot pussy flesh.

Liza groaned in pleasure, which encouraged Hilary. She wanted nothing more than to please her mistress. And she wanted her mistress to pleasure her in return. Their bodies were sweating and undulating in the sun, the warmth and light making their mutual desire that much richer. Hilary put her mouth to Liza's cunt and began to drink of her sweetness. She tasted the free-flowing juices and found her tongue, her mouth and lips probing deeper and deeper inside Liza's pussy. Liza was groaning now, and lifting her hips slightly to meet Hilary's mouth. Hilary felt the rocking motion grow more steady. She felt her own pleasures rush as her head was pushed deeply between Liza's legs and she tasted the salty sweet juice of the older woman's pussy. Her own body was trembling in riotous response, her pussy alive with sexual urgency.

Hilary was deep into her mistress' cunt, lapping away at the sweet hole and flicking her tongue on the protruding clitoris.

"Suck me there," Liza ordered. "Suck hard, now."

Hilary took all of the sweet meat into her mouth and pulled on it, drawing it inward and sucking the orgasm out of Liza's cunt.

"Yes, that's right," Liza said, as the orgasmic feeling began to tickle her pussy. "Here it is."

She shoved her cunt fully into Hilary's face, and the sex slave lapped away at the swollen cunt lips, licking up the final spurts of come juice, licking Liza's cunt clean.

It was taboo at this point in the training for Hilary to be allowed to have an orgasm. Liza could barely control her desire to let Hilary come. She was so close, so on the edge, her hot pussy just ready to burst in the mouth of a sweet lover.

As Hilary continued to lick Liza's cunt, Liza could see her rubbing herself discreetly, as if in automatic reaction to her deep sexual ache.

"That's enough," Liza heard herself say, just as Hilary seemed about to come. The young woman's cunt twitched with aching desire; she wanted it so bad.

Hilary was shocked, and her twitching pussy was on the verge of coming just from pleasuring her mistress. Suddenly, the light energy of sexual satisfaction turned to unfulfilled sexual tension. She'd hoped that Liza would return the gesture and suck the come from her and give her release.

"It's not that I don't want to," Liza said. "God, I do. But it's still not time. Just keep knowing that in the end, my cunt will be yours for the pleasing without restriction; and your cunt will be mine."

Hilary continued to caress Liza's thighs as the spasms slowly faded back into her body. As Hilary relaxed, Liza's thoughts began drifting to other places. It was only a brief respite, a tiny moment of escape, for soon she opened her eyes to gaze down at her beautiful young slave.

The Applicant

"You are remarkable, my dear," she said, rising so she sat only inches away from Hilary's heaving breasts and pulsing body.

"Thank you for at least allowing me to pleasure you," said Hilary, her eyes downcast.

Liza decided to give Hilary just a taste of what she could look forward to; she could not resist touching the young woman, and she began running her hands over her soft, damp skin, her fingers slipping between her wet thighs and around to her tender cunt.

"You are wet," she said, playfully fingering Hilary's pussy.

"Yes," said Hilary, praying to be relieved of the orgasm that was boiling just under her flesh, yet knowing it could be a long wait.

Liza continued to press her fingers inside Hilary's dripping pussy, teasing the throbbing flesh. Hilary closed her eyes and moaned, but as quickly as she felt the pleasure, Liza withdrew her hand.

"It is not yet your time," Liza reminded her.

Hilary's eyes snapped open with shame, for Liza was admonishing her for her presumptuousness.

"You must earn your pleasure," she said.

Hilary drifted back to the present, but could not get the morning's events off her mind. Everything she did, all her surroundings, reminded her of the small pleasure she had given to her mistress, and the pleasure her mistress had allowed her to give. As she slowly made her way toward the house, the evening shadows beckoned the night, somehow seeming to promise pleasure. She ached to have Liza's beautiful hands gently, firmly stroking her body. She imagined Liza's sharp tongue penetrating her with pleasure. She visualized Liza's face buried between her thighs, her tongue gingerly rimming her burning cunt-hole. Hilary was so hot, she desperately desired release.

Once back in her room, as Hilary began to dress, she glimpsed herself in the mirror. She gazed at the curves of her slim body and thought how she was a perfect contrast to her mistress. Her generous bosom and her small, tight nipples offset Liza's smaller breasts and larger aureoles. She gazed at her own nipples that stood nearly an inch from the softness of her flesh. She had never known a more sensual person than her mistress. Liza was a woman whose body was built for pleasure, and everything she did, every way in which she moved, suggested sexuality. It was as though she changed the atoms that whirled around her, even the air itself, so that everything in her presence exuded sexuality as well. That blatant sexual energy and aura made Hilary feel obsessed with desire. In her thoughts and daydreams she often found herself between Liza's legs, pleasuring the sweet pink meat of her mistress' hot cunt. Just conjuring up the image would bring the sweet scent of Liza to mind.

Hilary continued to gaze at herself in the mirror, at her small waist that bloomed into curvaceous hips, complementing Liza's more mature figure. She wanted to feel Liza's body pressed against hers.

Hilary pulled the black stretch pants over her long legs. There was nothing about her body that she could hide wearing these pants. Every curve of her body, every shapely innuendo was accented, each swell and crevice asking to be noticed. She slipped the black lace camisole over her head and enjoyed the sensation of the cool silk lightly teasing her nipples. The thin fabric hid little and accentuated the fullness of her breasts, the curve of their firm shape, and the erectness of her nipples. This is how Liza expected her to dress that night, and Hilary felt a little nervous in the clothing, for it was bolder than her

The Applicant

usual style. She completed her outfit with a pair of black stiletto-heeled leather pumps, shoes that Liza had left for her. When she glanced at herself in the mirror, she realized that she looked like a hooker. It was startling to realize that she had placed herself in such a vulnerable position, a situation in which she would be used by her mistress and her mysterious master in any way they deemed useful or pleasurable. She tingled at the thought of having crossed her own boundaries in order to seek the pleasure she really desired. She felt more alive than she had ever felt before.

When she descended to the dining room, her mistress spoke to her directly.

"The maid is waiting for you in the kitchen," Liza said.

On her order, Hilary moved quickly into the kitchen, catching only a brief glimpse of the dining room and its arrangement. It was a room out of every fantasy she'd ever read, with massive sideboards and crystal and silver glimmering in the yellow light of the chandelier. With its subdued opulence and the aroma of good food filling the room, it was a wealth of sensations beyond Hilary's ability to discern clearly. She did note two things, however. First, there were only three places set at the table. Second, there was a woman seated next to Liza. She was a large woman with long, gleaming red tresses and a voluptuous body that gave off the distinct carriage of authoritative sensuality. She wore a cream chiffon blouse that was so sheer Hilary had been able to glimpse her undulating breasts beneath the fabric. She could not help staring, and as Hilary passed silently by, the woman returned her gaze rather hungrily. She was also able to note that the woman had Liza's undivided attention.

Hilary returned to serve the two women dinner. As she reached to remove the redhead's plate, the woman grabbed Hilary's wrist.

"Stand up straight," she ordered.

Hilary moved back a foot and obeyed the command, knowing instinctively that it was expected of her. Liza sat impassively looking at Hilary, her silence affirming Hilary's need to comply.

"Undo your buttons," the woman barked.

Hilary undid the three buttons of her camisole, and the sheer cloth fell away. Her breasts spilled out and she resisted the urge to cover herself with her arms.

"Pinch them," the woman demanded.

Hilary reached up and grasped her nipples with either hand and pinched her nipples until they were hard.

"Harder."

She pinched them until they hurt.

"Come closer," she was told.

Hilary moved closer to the strange woman. The woman leaned forward and took her breasts in a tight grip. Hilary flinched with fear at the coldness in the woman's eyes and the cruel grin on her lips. Hilary's body raced with erotic fear, for she was frightened by this woman's intensity and her dark, commanding presence.

"Get on with you," the woman said suddenly and turned away from Hilary to resume her conversation with Liza.

There was an aura of intrigue that seemed to permeate the meal, as the two women exchanged provocative glances, giving Hilary the impression that there was something unique in their relationship that she did not understand. She guessed that she would soon know more, but she was still curiously

The Applicant

stumped by the third, unoccupied place at the table. Hilary placed plates of food at the setting, but no one joined the party. Oliver still had not appeared.

"We're finished with our dinner, my dear. We'll have our coffee in the small parlor," said Liza.

"Yes ma'am. And this third place?" Hilary asked, nodding toward the empty place setting.

"Oliver will be down when we are finished eating. Just leave it."

Hilary cleared the dishes and returned to receive further instructions.

"Bring the coffee and come with us." Liza motioned to a door on the opposite end of the dining room, away from the kitchen. As Hilary followed, carrying the tray, she found herself in a very small parlor indeed. It was furnished with vibrant floral patterns, both on the walls and covering a plump lounging chair and an overstuffed sofa. There were pillows strewn everywhere and yards of silk draped about the windows. It was like a dark little nest tucked away in a darker forest of sensations. A fragrance of ripe flowers perfumed the air that was warm and humid from the late spring sun, now all but disappeared from the sky.

Liza directed Hilary to a spot on some pillows on the floor. She was told to sit after she had poured coffee for the two rather regal women.

"Hilary will be here to serve you, Diana. I think that you will approve of my choice." There was a hint of uncertainty in Liza's voice that Hilary was unaccustomed to hearing.

"She's charming. A bit shy perhaps, but I should imagine we can make her more ... *bold*. After all, if she plans to stay, he will want someone aggressive enough to suit his needs, not to mention *mine*."

"She pleased me well this afternoon, and with little instruction."

"Have you had many women before?" Diana turned and asked Hilary.

Up until that moment, Hilary had felt like an outsider in their conversation, simply an object of perusal, an object of pleasure, and she found that this realization did not really disturb her; in fact in pleased her. It also seemed strange to Hilary that Liza was submissive to this stranger. It seemed that this woman took charge of the situation and Liza just seemed to be there to please much in the same way Hilary was.

"No. I haven't had any women before ... before today," Hilary replied.

"You are a wise young woman to understand your position so quickly—your *proper* position that is. I prefer women who are bright and capable of comprehending their position as readily as you seem to." As the woman spoke, she exuded a sexuality that was unmistakable. "Liza dear, how is that divine young man you were training. You know, the one you fuck so frequently?"

Liza smiled.

"He's still divine."

"Have you trained him to be submissive to any demands?"

"I'm afraid not," answered Liza. "He is much too much like Oliver. He will never let a situation get too far out of his control, even if he does consent to be my toy for the moment. One can never say how long these things will last before the situation gets dangerous."

"Has a randy spirit, does he? Well, I'll have to see what I can do with him sometime," said Diana. She sipped her coffee and stretched her long legs out in front of her. She was haughty and arrogant, but Hilary could not help admitting to herself that the

The Applicant

woman was gorgeous. She had a different kind of beauty than Liza's. Hilary responded more sensually to Liza, but Diana's sexuality was compellingly dangerous. The relationship between the two women confused her. They behaved like friends having a pleasant after-dinner conversation, yet she sensed there was something else between them. Liza seemed more reserved in Diana's presence, less sure of herself.

"Hilary, remove your pants and let me see your posterior," Diana said abruptly.

The instruction, like so many in this odd household, came as a bit of a surprise to Hilary. But the woman Diana did not feel it necessary to explain. She casually waited for the young woman to do her bidding.

Hilary rose and slowly began to remove her black tights. She was wearing nothing underneath, and the dampness in her crotch was evidence that she was ready for release from this bondage of anticipation.

"Turn around and bend over."

Hilary complied.

"Spread your feet apart and bend until your hands touch the floor," commanded Diana.

Hilary struck the pose that was demanded of her, and felt her body flush with embarrassment; she felt awkward, exposing herself thus in front of the beautiful, desirable women.

"Yes, Liza, she will do quite well. Her ass and anus will be delightful targets, not unlike your own."

The position was most uncomfortable as well as vulnerable, but the two women seemed to be content to look at Hilary's ass and discuss it with an air of detachment.

"Who gets her first?" Diana asked.

"That is for Oliver to decide," Liza replied.

"Yes, I'm sure he'll want to watch, if not actually be the one to christen this virginity." She gave Hilary's round ass one last longing gaze.

"You may rise," said Diana at last.

"Hilary," Liza continued as the young woman turned around, "retrieve your paddle for us. I am certain that Diana would take great pleasure in using it on you."

Hilary blushed. The anticipation of the blows once again reddening the soft flesh of her ass made her burn before they had even begun. She turned and silently left the room, retreating through another door that led into the front hallway. Walking through the large house naked as she was, Hilary felt conspicuous, though there seemed to be nobody to see her. She passed through the central hallway on her way to the morning room. Glancing through a crack in the dining room door, she briefly caught a glimpse of a man. His back was to her, so she was unable to see his face, although she was able to note that he held his squared shoulders in a most authoritative manner. Hilary's loins burned even hotter than before. She stood for a brief moment peering into the room, her eyes searching his back as if she were willing him to turn around and see her, so that she could at last come face to face with the man she knew was Oliver. She wondered if he could feel her presence, though she was still some distance from him. Could he feel the heat of her body the way she could feel his? It occurred to her that he was toying with her—that he knew she was there but elected not to turn and acknowledge her presence. She wanted to stay longer, but she knew that it would not be wise, so she pulled herself away from the doorway and hurried into the morning room, found the paddle, and quickly retraced her steps back to the

The Applicant

parlor. When she passed the dining room again, the man was gone.

"I think I want you over the stool," Diana demanded coldly, as the young woman returned to the room. "And on your knees. I want your flesh stretched very tight."

Hilary moved immediately to the stool, her knees sinking into the soft fabric. She could feel her senses rise, and the pleasurable fear of expectation washed over her. As soon as she had lowered herself over the stool so that her bosom was resting on the ground, her ass in the air, the blows came swiftly, without further words; Diana administered six quick strikes of the paddle. Her blows were twice the speed and strength of those given Hilary by Liza the day before. She winced and gasped aloud.

"There," Diana said, "you can get up. Let me see you. Turn around." Hilary rose and turned her back to the woman, whose eyes were still flashing with sexual heat. "I like that your bottom reddens well despite your dark skin."

She paused, and then with a frightfully authoritative voice she said, "Now Hilary, come here. I want you to eat me out. And you'd better do it well." Before Hilary could completely turn around, Diana was removing her skintight pants to reveal sumptuous thighs and a light-red–haired pussy already glistening and ready for sex. "Get down on your hands and knees, slave. I want you to crawl to me. Now!" Diana opened her legs wide, exposing her sex before Hilary. "I want that tongue lapping at me, deep inside me."

Hilary obliged, wondering at the unreality of her situation. She crawled toward the beautiful woman who was commanding her to give her pleasure, then put her lips eagerly to the woman's throbbing pussy.

She found her to taste distinctly different than her mistress; Diana's cunt was more spicy. She was brash and demanding, and she grabbed Hilary's hair and pushed the younger woman's face roughly in between her thighs.

"Eat me, you slut!" she cried, as Hilary began to furiously lap at her hole and her hardened pink clit. "Harder! Stick it in me harder!"

Hilary fucked her with her tongue, her mouth becoming sore, but she didn't want to disappoint, and so she continued to suck and lick Diana's hot cunt with relish. Just as she thought she could feel Diana's gyrations getting wilder, and Hilary thought that the woman was close to orgasm, Diana rammed her cunt harder than ever against Hilary's face. The younger woman worked her tongue in as deeply as she could and heard herself moaning with the pleasure she was getting from sucking this woman's come out of her.

Diana was really going wild, pressing her pussy against Hilary's face, rubbing her sex meat against the young woman while screeching out commands of "eat, suck, finger-fuck." Finally, Hilary positioned two fingers inside the wide opening of Diana's cunt and fucked her furiously, while simultaneously sucking on her clitoris; she could feel the crisis near, and sucked so hard that she was sure this gave Diana some pain—pain the woman seemed to love, for within moments the juice of excitement was squirting from the red-haired cunt.

"You bitch, you're making me come all over you, slut. Suck it up, suck it good. Ohhh, yes."

Diana finally let out a wild scream and bucked violently against Hilary's mouth. Her body shuddered for what seemed like a long time, and then there was deafening quiet; the only sound breaking the silence was their breathing.

The Applicant

"Stroke me now," ordered Diana. Hilary's hands rubbed the woman's tender thighs while Diana continued to shudder with the dying pleasure of her passion.

"Lie back on the pillows, my dear, let me see you take yourself," said Diana, suddenly changing moods. Hilary complied, but first looked over at Liza for approval. Liza nodded, somewhat hesitantly. She was glad to at least be able to relieve herself and hoped they'd actually let her come.

Lying back on the pillows, she spread her legs wide and deliberately. Hilary noticed how Liza fairly squirmed from her place on the couch as she watched, but her hands were bound, preventing her from engaging in the scenario. It seemed to Hilary that Liza had been commanded to remain a voyeur this evening.

Hilary slowly opened the plump, freshly shaved folds of her netherlips and exposed her pumped and glistening sex. She found her clit and began rubbing the throbbing pink button slowly. The fires within her body were rising steadily to a quick peak. She wanted these two women to touch her; she wanted their mouths on her cunt, on her mouth. But she knew this was not to be, and so she opened her legs and her pussy-lips wider and played with herself, offering up her body without shame for all of their pleasure. As Hilary's body rose in fever, her long fingers rubbed her pussy harder and faster, sometimes dipping deeper into the blushing folds of her cunt. She was near her peak, ready to let the pulsing of her body take control, when suddenly a hand reached out and stopped her. It was Diana's hand, but it was Liza who spoke.

"Hilary, you are dismissed for the evening." There was a distinct tension in her voice, and it took Hilary a few moments to regain some composure, for the tenseness of Liza's voice frightened her. Hilary felt rudely abused for the interruption of her own gratification, but she also knew that it had all been part of the plan. She looked at Liza with a desperate gaze, but found nothing in her mistress' eyes. Hilary longed for nothing more than to go to her and caress her, to kiss her, to taste her sweet pussy one more time. She longed to rub her own swelling mound against Liza's and to unleash her come on her mistress; her pussy was so hot it hurt. But she rose and obediently left the room as Diana said impatiently, "Be off with you!"

"You have chosen well, Liza," said Diana, after Hilary had departed.

"Thank you. I was certain she would prove worthy of our intentions."

"Yes, Oliver will be pleased."

"He already is."

"Is he now?" asked Diana with some curiosity. "Then it won't be long, will it?"

"No, I don't suspect that it will be long; he has such a taste for young sweet things like her," sighed Liza.

"Yes. But I assume he'll wait for a little while," said Diana. "Now it is time to attend to you, and I suspect Oliver has something devious in mind. He never calls me unless he does. This all must be very difficult for you, the training, all the anticipation. I know Oliver doesn't take well to being put off."

"Yes, Diana. I imagine it will be quite a night." Liza's voice was subdued.

Liza received Hilary in the morning room the next day. The air was fresh and cool, and Hilary felt revitalized by the deep sleep she had enjoyed. The day-

The Applicant

light was still filled with a light fog, and there was a heavy dew on the lawn. A cool breeze caressed her face and thighs. She was wearing nothing but a light shift that clung to her body's curves.

"You have had a most adequate beginning to your adventure here." Liza spoke rather cooly, and this disappointed Hilary. "I should think that you have had enough for one weekend. You may swim and relax, and leave for home at your leisure."

"Thank you," Hilary said, holding herself back from saying more.

"And I shall see you next weekend?"

"Oh yes!" Hilary replied.

"You will find your next stay here quite different from this one. I suspect you understand that there is nothing predictable within these walls."

Hilary nodded.

"I have something for you," said Liza, more gently now. "Open it when you get home."

"I will," the younger woman replied, taking the parcel from her mistress.

There was not a trace of emotion in Liza's face, and this confused Hilary greatly. She wanted nothing more than to understand this woman. She wanted to know everything about her. And most of all, Hilary wanted to be locked in a passionate embrace with her; she wanted Liza's hands and lips all over her body. But she realized that all her longings, all her secret desires, would have to wait.

CHAPTER IV

Four

"You will greet her tonight and bring her to me," Liza said to Stephen, as she pulled on her silk shirt.

His bed in the upper room of the carriage house was mussed, just as everything else about the room was a masterpiece of disarray. The floor was stacked with books, the table littered with papers and empty beer bottles. The sink was filled with dishes, and hastily plucked field flowers were jammed into a jar at the windowsill. Stephen's clothes were thrown here and there, but his sheets were clean. They were always clean and fragrant with the smell of outdoors that came in with them from the line.

She pulled him close to her once more, devouring his luscious cock in her mouth. She pulled his prick to her with both hands, and bent down over the beautiful rod, kissing, then licking the pink-purple head; it was hard as a rock and she loved the feel of his youthful, swollen cock in her mouth, in her hands, in her pussy.

His big hands went to her head and ran his fingers through her hair, stroking her like he would a puppy. "Good girl," he was saying, groaning in pleasure. "Oh, you make Stephen's cock so hard, so big."

She was burning up inside, her cunt growing more moist, her nipples standing on end. She rubbed up and down the shaft with one hand and she fondled his balls with the other. He groaned even louder and she began to tease him, rimming the head of his cock with her tongue, running it over the head, along the underside, down the shaft to the balls, where she took one, then the other deeply into her mouth and sucked.

"Suck him," Stephen begged. "Suck my little man and make him cry with joy."

Liza took his hardened cock deeply into the warmth of her mouth in a truly submissive manner, following Stephen's instructions and pleasuring him in ways that made him wiggle and writhe and thrust his cock deeper into her mouth.

"Now you're doing it," he was groaning. "Now you're giving my cock a good ride in your mouth." He punctuated his sentence by pounding it further, deeper, into her open expert orifice. His hardness was rubbing against her teeth, the roof of her mouth, close to her throat; he pumped away while pulling her head closer.

"You're making ... it ... come," he stammered, as the first gush of orgasm erupted into Liza's mouth. "Drink it all up and lick it clean," he said, practically thrusting himself down her throat as the last drip of come shot out of him.

The Applicant

She swallowed him whole and drank up his juices. She licked her lips, and with her tongue washed his entire cock, licking up every trace of his dew. It was still hard and Stephen was still desirous. He wanted to fuck her; he wanted to take her standing; he wanted to bend her over and ram his rod deep into her female place and fill her up with his still-hard cock; he wanted to rub his groin against hers, press deliciously on her clitoris, finger her asshole, and suck her tits in the way he knew would make her cunt explode with pleasure—pleasure that kept her bonded to him, for Liza loved the pleasure she knew in his bed.

But her pussy had other things to do. As wet as it was, and as much as her flesh was willing, she could not stay. She loved his youthful, hard body; she loved his arrogance and unwillingness to be totally controlled; she loved the way he was always pure man; and she loved the beautiful cock from which she had just siphoned the sex juices—but she had to get going.

He came after her, his hands groping at her breasts, her ass, her cunt; he was hungry for more and it seemed like he would take it. He grabbed her wrists hard.

"Fuck me, lady of the house," he said, a sexy smile sliding across his beautiful tanned face. "Let me have that juicy cunt once again. Let me get inside and make your pussy sing. Open your legs." He pulled at her arm to make her stay. "Open for me."

He was still smiling, cooing, as he begged her to give her pussy to him again. But she pushed him away with a playful slap.

"No, twice is enough for you. After all, you will have your pleasure in these next few days." She pulled herself out of the deep bed and found her shoes.

"You want her in the stable house or the tack room?" he said with a sly smile.

"In the morning room," Liza said carefully.

"Oh," replied Stephen in mock disappointment.

"I think this weekend will be unlike anything you have ever seen before, even at this nasty estate," she said with a devious twinkle in her eye.

His eyebrows raised in curiosity.

"She is quite special to you, isn't she?" he remarked.

"Do I detect a note of jealousy?"

"Why should I be jealous?" he said. "After all, I get all the sex I want." She heard his sarcasm, and it displeased her.

"She must be primed and ready for Oliver when he wants her," Liza said curtly. "Though I don't think it will happen this weekend; it's too premature."

"Much too busy with you, is he?"

She flashed a quick glare at him.

"I'd love to see your rump hoisted again," he snickered, egging her on.

She stood to leave.

"I think you'll be quite busy with Hilary."

"I only wish she were as enamored of me as she is of you," he said, as he pulled a pair of well-worn jeans over his hips and tucked his beautifully formed cock away.

"Oh, I think she appreciates you. I can't imagine anyone not appreciating you," Liza said, softening her stare at Stephen.

"You mean the way Diana appreciates me?"

"Diana would probably love to fuck you, or rather she would love it if you fucked her. I'm sure she needs it. I sure she's positively green with envy that I have *two* beautiful men to screw."

"Yes, I guess so—with all the lovers that you man-

The Applicant

age to string along, anyone would be intimidated." He stared at her a long time, and Liza smiled at him cruelly.

"I guess we're stuck with each other; unless of course you'd like to leave. You're free to go anytime you'd like, you know."

But before he could answer, she dashed out the door and down the stairs, turning to wave at him from the lawn below. And then she turned again and made her way up the hill.

Stephen watched her until she disappeared into the house. He finished dressing, his mind and loins churning in anticipation of Hilary's arrival.

"Come in. You can leave your things at the door—you won't be needing them," Stephen said. He couldn't help thinking how innocent she looked—and how vulnerable and young.

Hilary hadn't expected Stephen to greet her. She had hoped it would be Liza, though seeing his virile body charged her entire being; everything in the house had that effect on her—the sights, the scents, the sexual energy that permeated the place.

She left her bags at the door and followed him through the hall into the morning room where Liza sat. Her mistress looked radiantly seductive—on fire but content. She looked liked she did when Hilary had first met her. When Hilary had last seen her, she'd been so quiet and withdrawn. And now, there she sat, posed like royalty in her chair.

"Please stand, Hilary," she instructed.

"Yes," the young woman obeyed, positioning her luscious flesh in front of her female lover.

"I promised that this weekend will be unlike the last, and certainly like no other you will experience. You say you desire to be a submissive?"

"Yes." Hilary looked down Liza, her heart pounding with anticipation.

"Then you will know submission. It will be far beyond anything you expected. You will truly know the meaning of the word. If you flinch more than a second at any demand, if you disobey any command, if you cry out in protest even once, you will be removed from this house so fast your head will be reeling. Do you understand?"

"Yes." She was crawling with fear and excitement inside.

"Lest you fear too much my dear, this weekend is not designed to hurt you, but to give you pleasure as you learn your proper place and enjoy in pleasing sexually anyway you are asked."

Liza's eyes were steely cold. Hilary longed to see the warmth she'd known from them in the past. But there was not a glimmer of affection in her mistress' eyes. Yet Hilary trusted this woman and this game that they were acting out. Her body was nearly spasming with orgasm as Liza spoke to her with such a commanding voice—a voice shrill and authoritative. The sound of that voice reached down to a depth within her, to that place where her secrets lay, and her desire to be completely submissive. Hilary knew that she would do anything Liza commanded, that she was owned and a slave to whatever situation would transpire in the next few days and nights.

"You will be blindfolded the entire weekend. You will be served, as you will be unable to serve yourself. Speak only if your body requires elimination, and say only, 'I must go.' Nothing more. Do you understand?"

"Yes."

"Stephen, blindfold her. She will wait here until the others arrive."

The Applicant

Liza quickly departed the room with no further instructions. Stephen had observed the scene from some several feet away. He had watched impassively, his arms crossed, waiting for his further instructions. When Liza left the room, he moved forward slowly and removed a blindfold from his pocket. He dropped it on a chair and went to a cabinet and drew out a pair of handcuffs.

"This first," he said, and approached Hilary. He pulled her arms behind her where he fastened her wrists firmly. She could feel the warmth of his body so close to hers, and she felt exposed as her breasts were forced to be thrust out by her new position with her hands behind her back. Hilary could feel Stephen's crotch against her thigh, and his hands took the liberty of roving underneath her short skirt. He roughly pulled Hilary's moistened panties from her body. "Hmmmm," he smiled as he withdrew them, noting how ready for sex she had become.

"I'd like to bend you over and fuck you right now," he said. "Too bad you won't be able to see all the pleasures ready and waiting for you," he continued, as he carefully placed the blindfold about her eyes. He pulled it tight; though it was not uncomfortable, it was not likely to slip.

"If this doesn't stay on, I'll be exchanging it for the full mask."

He led her to a corner of the room and ordered, "Sit down." She lowered herself carefully to a low stool, allowing Stephen to keep her from falling down in awkwardness. Once seated, Stephen's strong hands spread her legs and raised her skirt so that her pussy was completely exposed. She could feel the tingle of fresh air caress her exposed sex, and the warmth of Stephen's hands on her thighs charged her skin with desire. She hoped he would continue to play with her body, but he didn't. Instead, he carefully arranged her arms behind her back. From behind, he leaned over her and undid the buttons of her dress and pulled out her breasts. The massage of his hands aroused her already erect nipples even more, and she leaned into his caress. She tried to reach to him with her face, to lick his neck or stroke his arm with her cheek, for she wanted to arouse him, she wanted him to desire her.

"You are quite tempting, Hilary, but we are not each other's to have. I am leaving now."

Hilary heard him turn on his heel and walk away. For a moment she felt rather panicked at having been left here alone, bound, blindfolded, and completely exposed, but her fear swiftly turned into a kind of erotic trepidation. She began the long wait.

The swiftness of her reentry into Liza's erotic world left her exhilarated and frightened. It had seemed a long, drawn-out week since her last visit. Her mind raced back to the first night that she returned home. She threw down her bag and quickly opened the package from Liza. Inside there was a single item: a collar. It was made of soft tooled leather, and she held it to her face, to her cheek. She brought the black collar to her nose and smelled the richness of the leather, and that smell made her body sting with strange excitement.

"Wear it in the evening, during the night, whenever you are alone, ... to remind you of your servitude."

The note inside the package had been simple, and Hilary had followed the instructions carefully. She wore the collar whenever she was alone, and she had worn it that evening when she had returned to the estate.

As she sat in the chair, Hilary thought about how

The Applicant

she had awakened every night, the tightness of the leather around her neck bringing her out of sleep. The leather collar fed her fantasies that kept her awake for hours, and at last she would fall asleep in the early morning. She was exhausted at work, but the thoughts of Liza and the estate kept her steadily moving toward the end of the week. Her hands were often between her thighs, her fingers stroking the lips of her cunt, teasing her clit lightly and then more violently. But per her mistress' instructions, she never made herself come when Liza was not present to watch; she would never cheat on her lover in that way. She would lie in her own tub and reminisce about the sensuous bath that she had enjoyed the previous weekend. It was hard for her to eat because she was so preoccupied. It seemed that the collar around her neck at dinnertime symbolized her submission, and she ate as if her mistress was watching over her.

She enacted a ritual every evening when she came home from work. She would stand naked in front of her mirror and clinically observe her body; she would admire the curve and nudity of her shaved pussy. She would wrap the collar around her neck, snapping it so that it fit tightly. She could have worn it more loosely, but she knew that a proper submissive would wear the collar snug, and so must she. She spent her week suspended in another world, yet she knew she was not completely in that world; still, the world of her life before seemed utterly different and strange.

And then at last she returned to the estate and found herself sitting in the house of her dreams and nightmares. There she sat, clothed in the collar, on display for her mistress, her mistress' lover, the house servants. She was on display for anyone that passed by.

It seemed like hours, and was at least that long as she sat on the low stool. She began to feel as though she had been forgotten in the corner of the morning room. She tried to relax in the late sun of the afternoon, and then the warmth was gone, and she heard the clock strike twice. A fly chose to light on her leg, and it seemed an eternity before it flew away. A cool breeze stroked her body from an open window, and the air stroked her naked pussy as it lay exposed.

Other than these periodic physical distractions, Hilary was lost in her waiting world, oblivious to most everything else. She focused mostly on her desires, thoughts that did not come to her in specific form but rather swam about her consciousness in a montage of uncertainties and fears. What if she were to be beaten and her body could not withstand it? Would she not cry out? Would they stop? Yet as her mind filled with apprehension, her body was on fire and her cunt wet and ready.

Sometime after the clock struck eight, and Hilary had been sitting for nearly three hours on the stool, an unknown pair of hands unclasped her hands from behind her back. Soft sensuous fingers unloosed her bonds and massaged her fingers and wrists, which had grown numb. She was then lifted by gentle, womanly hands, and with a strange arm about her waist, she was led to a bathroom where she was allowed to relieve herself.

But to her dismay, she was returned to the morning room and bound again. She was placed in another chair; one with arms and legs to which her limbs were strapped. The top of her dress was loosened once again, and her skirt was lifted over her thighs, so that anyone who might pass would see her completely exposed. Hilary craved more; she craved those sensuous hands to invade her, to tease and slap her breasts; those fingers to find the wet insides of her cunt and pleasure her. But she was required once more to wait.

CHAPTER V

Five

The noise was startling in its suddenness. At once a rush of activity was crashing in on her languid body, disrupting the quiet of her suspended state. A swarm of hands and breath and bodies pulled her from near sleep, and like a sudden storm they carried her away. Her heart and head were pounding with the rapid change. Quite suddenly, Hilary found that her clothes had been removed by the active hands. She wore only the collar around her neck and this added to her feeling of complete helplessness, a feeling that she had been wishing to experience for a long time. She was lead up some stairs and into a warm, humid room. Hilary realized she was in the bathroom, and the next thing she knew she was gently pressed into a deep bath of hot, fragrant water.

Somehow, Hilary could sense Liza's watchful gaze, and the thought stirred her body, her loins and her imagination. Hilary cautiously sank back into the water and it surrounded her like liquid silk. Soon enough she felt and heard other bodies climbing into the bath, which was large enough to hold them all. She began to feel their hands caressing her flesh, attending to her body, and with some concentration, she was able to discern that there were a pair of male hands and a pair of female hands slowly washing her aching flesh. They washed her breasts, and with delicate tongues licked her erect nipples. The body that was definitely male took Hilary's nipple between his teeth and gave her a ferocious little nip that made her quiver and nearly cry out, but she stifled her cry because she remembered that it was forbidden. She felt the more feminine pair of hands massaging her arms and chest and back, and soon she was nearly faint with the pleasure of such succulent caresses. After a period of time that seemed altogether too short to Hilary, a pair of hands gently urged her from the water, and she complied with the silent command. As she stood, hands began to rub her body with a beautiful-smelling oil, and as the hands worked the oil into her tender flesh, they took the liberty of lightly fingering her sex, and the untouched hole of her anus. Someone began to prod her more deeply, entering her asshole with a curious finger, and she began to moan with delight. As the finger entered her more deeply, she gasped with pain, which was quickly followed by a rush of excitement that darted to every corner of her body. The finger moved rapidly in and out, and with each movement her body convulsed. Hilary felt that she was falling out of control, and she didn't care at all.

At last she was led to a table where she was gently

The Applicant

pushed down on soft terry towels. She allowed her thoughts to vanish so that she could concentrate on the sensual pleasure of the massage she was receiving. Hands moved down her body, rubbing deeply into the back of her thighs, the soft flesh of her buttocks, and the sinewy lines of her graceful back. A drop of creamy chocolate was placed on her tongue, and like every other sense engaged at the moment—every other sense but sight—the candy dissolved into another wordless bit of ethereal pleasure. Music played softly, emanating from somewhere above, and the sound held her in a melody of tranquility that she hoped would not end.

She was gently turned so that her most sensitive parts were exposed, and the caresses became more intense. Her breasts were rudely squeezed, and then touched with a feather lightness that made her arch her back to meet the touch hungrily. Her belly churned, and the hands that touched it tenderly caressed it more violently as well. And then the hands and curious fingers found their way to her sweet sex, and they began to tease her. At first the touch was light, almost imperceptible; then more and more rapid. Hilary's body bucked and writhed, her groans becoming part of the music in the room. It seemed as though everything, even the damp air, were caressing her, and everything seemed to soothe her. Everything she was experiencing was sending her to a world far away from any world she'd ever known before.

She drifted inside herself, her body still spasming, sending little messages to her lovers. Yet they were not done with her, and the hands carried her from the table to cushions, pillows, and soft, silky comforters that cradled each part of her body.

Liza stood in the corner of the exquisite room,

watching the bodies on the cushions begin to very slowly move together in the dim candlelight. Stephen stood behind her, and his hands began to remove her clothing as he, too, watched the wonderful natural drama of sexual play on the cushions of the room. He reached into Liza's tissue-thin silk blouse and squeezed her tits. As he bit her neck, his other hand found its way to her crotch and began to finger her wet pussy feverishly. Neither Liza nor Stephen took their eyes from the writhing bodies in the center of the room.

Hilary, lying on her back, was the centerpiece of the sexual tableau; but she was by no means a passive receiver in the passion that was being acted out. In swift measure her mouth was greeted by a young man's large, engorged cock, while a young woman lay over her, rubbing pussy to pussy in furious rhythm. The two women's breasts brushed against one another as their hips gyrated wildly. Liza watched the woman between Hilary's legs and felt her own pussy contract with desire. She pressed Stephen's hand further up her cunt, as she watched the two women's shaved flesh meet in glistening union. It was a playground that Liza would have readily joined. Her desires for Hilary were so charged that it was all she could do not to pull Stephen into the fray of the orgy going on before them. But she was bound by rules that were not of her own making, and she had been commanded to simply watch. Liza realized that there was no greater aphrodisiac than forced time and distance between the initial spark of passion and its final fiery fruition.

As the women rubbed each other, Hilary thrust her cunt hard against the woman on top of her. Her hips pressed forward, silently begging for more and more penetrating sensations. She could feel their

The Applicant

juices mixing. She could feel the folds of their individual sexes fusing together as they worked each other toward that ecstatic rush that would send them out of their bodies for a brief, flaming moment of orgasmic bliss.

The cock in Hilary's mouth grew larger, and the man, growing more passionate, thrust his member deeper and deeper into her mouth, down her throat. She choked, but her persistent lover did not relent in his intention to spill his jism down her throat.

It was poetry to Liza's eyes, watching Hilary being possessed at either end, giving and receiving her pleasure. Hilary seemed like a vessel of sex and nothing more, and the thought made Liza burn with desire. What things she imagined for her young slave. What wild pleasurable tortures she had in mind for her lover.

As the three bodies rose in a wave of mutual pleasure, they began preparing themselves for the final thrusts that would bring them to orgasm. Their bodies seemed to rise in such expectation that it seemed the level of tension could rise no higher, and one by one they began to spill over into the darkness of ecstasy. Hilary was lost, her mind gone as her body became the vehicle to carry her to orgasm. The woman over Hilary arched her back, pressing her cunt hard against Hilary's, and she began rocking back and forth screaming out with pleasure, just as the young man spilled himself over Hilary's lips, bathing her face with his orgasm.

But this was no ending; it was only the start of many more scenes in the wild drama that Liza had orchestrated. There was another man and woman who had been toying with one another, watching and waiting for their turn with Hilary's beautiful body. They approached Hilary, and the striking young man, who was already erect, turned Hilary on her her hands and knees. Her cunt was exposed perfectly, still glowing with the juice of her recent orgasm. The second young man wasted no time and thrust his engorged cock into her quivering pussy. Stephen could no longer simply stand by and watch.

"Will you be joining us?" he whispered to Liza.

"You know I can't," she said breathlessly.

"Poor you. This is too good to pass up."

"Yes," she said, "poor me. But the waiting is so delicious."

Stephen chuckled quietly, and without hesitation moved forward to join the wonderful grouping of bodies on the floor. He licked and sucked Hilary's fingers while the man who rode her brought himself to a delicious explosion, and then Stephen prepared to enter her. But first, he bent his face between her trembling thighs and licked her inner pussy-lips up and down, finally dipping his tongue into her hole to clean out the male jism and sex juice that was building like a dam inside her. Only then was he ready to fuck her.

It became Hilary's task to please all her faceless lovers at once, all the participants furiously finding a way to satisfy themselves. Yet Stephen reigned king for a while, shoving his big shaft deep into her aching, twitching opening and pulling it outward in slow, sensual, teasing motions. He pressed his big cock deep inside her again and she received him with great pleasure. At the same time, her mouth was alternately fed cunts and cocks so that she was quite thoroughly engaged in pleasing them all. Her hands grasped at cocks that offered themselves to her caresses, and her fingers teased and stroked pussies that presented themselves to her for service. With each lick, stroke, and thrust, she brought them all closer to completion.

The Applicant

Stephen was tearing her in two as he shoved his cock further and further inside her, and her back arched with pleasure as much as with pain. In her hand a cock erupted shooting sperm over her hand and arm. Immediately a cunt was writhing on her sperm-wet hand, and soon the woman was riding her finger wildly. And then Stephen was coming inside her, pumping her full of his come, as another woman shoved her hot pussy onto Hilary's welcoming lips. Hilary sucked on the woman's clit, and licked her cunt as if she were a trained pro. She was devouring the woman's writhing love-opening just as Stephen shot the last of his load. After all had been fulfilled, they collapsed into an exhausted heap on the floor.

The players sank into the softness of the comforters and pillows, their bodies entwining as they lay quietly resting. And Liza watched, her body filled with unspent need; she was burning, aching inside. She wanted to dive in to all that available flesh; she wanted them to hold her down and fuck her wildly. She longed to lie down on the pillows, spread her legs wide, and expose her wet, hungry cunt—to leave herself open for tongues, and lips, and cocks. She measured her breathing, and let go of her immediate desires. If she did join in, she would be transgressing. And the pain of a transgression was enough to keep her from misbehaving.

As a calm descended on the room, the breathing of the lovers becoming easy and deep, *he* appeared.

He didn't say a word, though his figure was imposing and cut through the easy peace like a dark rumbling of thunder. They all looked in his direction, as Oliver's eyes keenly combed the room. All eyes were on him—all eyes save Hilary's. He held his hand out to Liza, for clearly no other command was needed.

Liza rose quickly from her cushions and took his hand. He continued to stare at the bodies in the room, at the players of the recent drama. And then, suddenly, he turned and left the room, taking Liza with him.

CHAPTER VI

Six

They had fucked until dawn and then lay down to a peaceful sleep. They woke to a late-morning sun streaming in through the windows. They woke to the smell of warm, fragrant food that had been silently delivered to their den of delight.

Hilary wanted to greet the morning with her eyes. She wanted nothing more than to actually see the beautiful bodies that had afforded her so much pleasure the night before. But she remained blindfolded, committed to the instructions her mistress had given her. The pressure of her body's needs demanded that she find the toilet. Yet she was afraid to speak, lest she break the spell of the previous night's enchantments. Finally, she said, "I must go," and she found it strange to hear her own voice, the sound of it locating her body in reality.

To her surprise, she felt a man's hand leading her to the toilet which was nothing more than a chamber pot in one corner of the room. A hint of embarrassment passed through her, for she had never urinated in front of a man before.

"Play with yourself as you piss," he said.

With some little hesitation, she reached between her legs. She would not violate the rules by refusing, yet something made her want to shout out "NO!" Instead, she sat over the pot and spread her legs. As the warm rush of relief flooded from her body, she put her fingers to her red clit. Some of the warm liquid streamed down over her fingers, and it was a wonderful sensation. She began to relax, enjoying the simultaneous sensations of relief and titillation. But as soon as she began to enjoy it, his voice said, "That's enough." She suddenly recognized him. It was Stephen.

"You're becoming the perfect submissive," he said, "but today will really test your commitment. Don't flinch in the face of fear."

His words sent shocks of danger through her body as she stood. But she wanted more; Hilary looked forward to darker things. Though last night had been wonderfully sensual, she craved things that her imagination would not even allow her to envision.

No sooner had she been returned to the center of the room when a pair of hands led her from the room altogether. They thrust her into an icy bath, the water so cold that it shocked her. It took a while before she could catch her breath as deep shivers ran through her body. The hands lathered her with a thick soap and scrubbed her body vigorously. Her skin was roughed up a bit so that when an ointment was applied to her skin afterward, it stung as thought nettles had been pressed into her flesh.

The Applicant

It was an afternoon of contrasts, one imposed rudely upon another in mysterious succession. After her bath, she was lifted from the water and taken on another journey through the house. She was guided down what seemed to be an interminable flight of stairs. There was a dampness surrounding her that suggested that she was in the cellar, but she wasn't sure, and this uncertainty made her fearful.

After a moment's pause, having reached the bottom of the stairs, she was pushed against a rough stone column. Her feet were spread wide to either side of the structure, and her hands were pulled around the column and tied securely so that she was hugging it. A leather belt was placed tightly around her waist to further secure her. After this flurry of activity, Hilary was left alone.

She shivered as she felt the cold stinging her pores, and she longed for the comforting touch of the now-familiar hands. She knew that they were not far away, for she could hear them. Waiting to be touched was torture far more excruciating than any roughness or pain.

The others were waiting in the dank basement for Liza to join their company. She would arrive and direct them, and they knew from experience the course that the afternoon would take. They lay quietly against the pillows that had been arranged for them, lounging in one another's arms, watching Hilary's exposed body with pleasure.

"Your bitch is ready for you," Stephen said, as he leaned against the doorframe that led into Liza's bedroom.

"Feel free to come right in without asking." Liza said sarcastically.

"Door was open," he replied irritably.

She sat back against the cushions of her bed, her body seductively exposed to his view.

"You're awfully cool this afternoon," she said. "What's wrong with you? Jealous?"

"No, I am not jealous. I'm not in the mood to spar with you, Liza," he said, almost as a warning.

"I think this room upsets you, because you know that this is where Oliver and I fuck."

"This room does not upset me," he said curtly.

"Well," she said in a low voice, "we've never fucked here."

"The opportunity has never presented itself," he said.

She laughed, looking at him with a taunting gleam in her eye. Her body was exuding an animal heat, and simply being near her was making his loins burn. The way she was moving toward him, catlike, on the bed, was an invitation to join her.

"I want your cock inside me," she said, her voice lowered to a growl. "I want to feel you inside me, thrusting hard." She could see anger in his eyes, and resentment that she was possessed by another. She knew inciting his anger was dangerous, but the opportunity was too compelling to resist.

"Fuck me," she said.

He moved rapidly toward the bed, his anger giving in to his lust, and he took her roughly by the shoulders. Her threw her down hard against the mattress and opened her legs wide with his hands to glimpse her juicy, wet cunt. He pulled out his cock and without hesitation thrust himself hard into her, driving into her deeply with all his might. He pinned her down with his own body as she began to resist his violent thrusts. Stephen didn't want her to have any pleasure—he only wanted to take from her and leave her writhing in the sheets, begging him for more. He was fucking her hard and fast, one thrust following another with a force that was gaining in violence. She

The Applicant

screamed and moaned and he slapped her face and her breasts.

"Shut up! You can only play with me so long, and then you're mine."

He pushed his cock into her deeper and deeper, so that his pubic hair was rubbing hard against her own hairless mound. Before Liza knew it, Stephen was spewing his load deep in her womb. As quickly as he had entered her, he withdrew his gleaming shaft.

"There. I fucked you," he said. And then pushing his cock back in his pants, he turned and left Liza on the bed.

Had she been alone, Liza would have quickly finished what Stephen had started, but when she looked up to watch Stephen go, she saw *him* standing in the doorway watching her coldly.

Oliver's coldness charged her soul.

"There are consequences for your actions," he said.

Liza turned away. She could not stand his dark eyes penetrating her as they did. She knew she would pay the price for her indiscretion, and in some part of her mind she wanted nothing more than to pay. Oliver was her master, and he would mete out any punishment that he saw fitting.

Hilary stood bound to the column for hours. This time her wait was far less comfortable than it had been in the chair. Her legs began to tremble with weakness, and her wrists were aching. She couldn't help wondering what lay ahead for her, and she contemplated the dark places that her captors would most likely take her. As the aching in her body increased, she realized she would do anything to have those faceless hands touching her body again. She didn't care what form the caresses took, whether they were soft or firm, rough or tender. She simply wanted the human contact. She began to wonder if she would ever be attended to again.

When at last it did begin, she almost didn't notice, so light and delicate were the caresses she received.... They were running feathers over her body, and the whispering touch of them tantalized her and reminded her of her own body, of the pleasure or pain that was about to come. The play of feathers made every inch of her flesh tingle, made her body more attentive to the waiting. Her inner fires were just beginning to burn, and her desire was mounting—her desire for experiences more intense and dark. As soon as she began to consider this, her flesh was greeted by the harsh reality of the smell of leather. The smell filled her nostrils, and as she recognized the animal smell of the leather, the cool surface of the material moved across her flesh. It caressed the tender portions of her body and that wicked place where pleasure becomes torture. She writhed against the cold stone pillar. The leather straps began to wind their way around her upper body, around her tits and over her shoulders. The sensations consumed her attention. It was a greater anticipatory pleasure than she had ever known. Suddenly a stark object pierced through her pleasure, as a new instrument was delicately smoothed down her spine. The object did not have the flexibility or malleability of the leather; it was cold, hard, and smooth. And suddenly this cool object made its way down the crack of her ass, and she realized what was happening to her. She cried out, startled by the realization that it was some sort of leather whip. Her body jerked against her bonds, and she thrust forward against the stone between her legs, causing the whip to press ever so slightly against her sweetly puckered ass orifice.

The Applicant

Her whole body was on fire, caught in the crossroads of extreme sexual heat and passion, and fear of the unknown. Her clitoris was swelling and her nipples were getting harder as her asshole was teased with the hard leather whip.

She was wanting the pain that would come with the pleasure of this experience; her body longed for the contrast of pain and pleasure to merge into one and empower her to great sexual heights. She was choosing the experience that was to come; she was choosing to be submissive and to accept whatever would come next. Just the anticipation of danger made the waves of pleasure rise in her pussy and envelop her very being.

It was then that the rough play began. Hilary did not experience cruel blows; but a repetition of light lashes with the leather whip enticed her flesh, urging her to cry out for more. She craved the quick charge that dared to send her body over the edge of delight because of this torment. Blows rained upon her thighs, on her ass, on her legs. Each lash was so well placed, there was no way for Hilary to guess or anticipate the next meeting of leather with her flesh.

There were two administrators of this punishment; and it was punishment that Hilary interpreted as excruciating pleasure. Behind the reins of this sensual game of thrill and terror were a man and a woman, artfully administering the blows upon Hilary's vulnerable body. Surprisingly, the woman's strokes were more intense, more focused than the man's; the woman's lashes lightly bruised Hilary's soft flesh. The woman concentrated mostly on Hilary's ass and thighs while the man flicked his tasseled buggy whip over most of her body with soft strokes. Like a play of light and dark against her body, the heat rose wildly inside her; Hilary's flesh was at last coming alive.

She wanted to let free the pleasure that was stuck in her throat; she wanted to scream and moan and thrust herself in orgasm against the stone column. As she writhed, she rubbed her cunt against the jutting stone, and her body came closer and closer to another orgasm. She pulsed in rhythm, allowing the instruments of her passion to increase her curious pleasure. Hilary's body jumped and jerked in a purposeful way against the stone until the fury of her movements amplified so that she pulled up tight, every muscle within her being tensing in a final wave of pleasure. A warm wave of sexuality cascaded from deep within her. For a moment, she felt suspended in time; then she finally screamed and wailed like an animal in heat, her orgasm falling free from her lips.

Her body hung limp and weak, her backside splotched and red from the punishment. She continued to jerk softly, undulating again and again against the stone pillar that had been warmed by the heat of her body. At last she relaxed against her bonds as she felt the last trickle of pleasure drift away. She was too tired to keep herself supported, so the hands were obliged to lay her out on a soft mattress. Her body delighted in the comfort of the soft cushion beneath her. But her relief was not long-lasting, for as soon as she was laid down, her legs were parted and she was tied spread-eagle across the mattress, her face toward the low ceiling of the cellar.

The faceless company that had surrounded Hilary now prepared to *take* pleasure from her ultimately submissive body. A large cock suddenly thrust into her mouth; the member was not introduced gently but rudely, completely opening her mouth until it stretched to the point of pain. At the same time another man's cock entered her cunt, and she was fucked hard and fast at both ends. Neither man tried

The Applicant

to please her; rather, they were solely interested in taking their pleasure as they wished. The women, whose hands caressed her roughly, pinched her nipples hard between their fingers and took little love bites from her belly and tit flesh.

It was a show that grew more fierce each moment. Every act, every thrust, every bite was more wild. It was a tableau to bring a gleam to Liza's eye. She walked into the cellar just as the building passion was reaching its heated apex. It was as if when Hilary climaxed, Liza came too. As the men thrust deeply into Hilary's passive body, Liza felt jolts of submissive delight. It reminded Liza of herself in the not-too-distant past. Hilary lay there, her body like a ripe fruit, open and waiting to be plucked. She was going to be the perfect toy for Liza's imaginative and rapacious desires. Oh yes, Liza would wait as she was required, knowing that the waiting was an important part of the seduction. Liza watched jealously as Hilary dutifully, and clearly joyfully, licked out the pussies that were thrust over her tongue after the men had taken their pleasure.

The first woman had a tall, slim body and a bright pink cunt with a very wet opening; it looked like cherry candy. She had been fingering herself while watching the men take Hilary, so her cunt was very wet and engorged and she was on the edge of exploding.

Hilary tongue-fucked her pussy like she was a pro, parting the pink lips with her fingers, spreading the opening with a flat tongue and diving into the cunt meat with delicious, long, slurping strokes. The woman was so beside herself with pleasure that she had her legs spread totally open and was holding her own pussy-lips open. Liza longed to be the woman who was at that moment receiving the attentions of Hilary's tongue.

"Oh yes, very good," the woman was groaning. "Get that tongue all the way in my cunt. Tongue-fuck me. Lash me with your tongue. Do my clit now ... faster ... lick hard ... suck it, yes." The commands were endless, and Hilary met them all until the woman finally settled on being sucked off with one finger pressed up her cunt and another in her asshole.

Hilary gently sucked on the swollen clit bud to tease and increase the cunt heat, and then pressed one finger into the wet pussy-hole. She rubbed a second finger in there, collecting the juice that would oil the other opening. Then she slipped her finger into the tight, puckered asshole.

The woman bucked beneath her, so Hilary fucked good and hard; she rammed the woman with her fingers and began to suck harder on the bursting clit bud.

"That's right, that's right ... yes," the woman screamed, her hips trembling as Hilary's lips lapped away at her exploding cunt. With the orgasm complete, Hilary still held the woman's trembling thighs apart. "Lick it clean," the woman ordered. And Liza watched as her sweet submissive eagerly lapped at the cunt before her, cleaning it of jism and renewing the vigorous passion it had displayed moments ago.

Every woman had something licked or sucked or fingered by Hilary; and there were no complaints about her abilities. The only complaint was that Liza's cunt was in overdrive from the excitement of watching her lover-slave between the legs of the other women. She watched, burning inside, as a young woman turned around and thrust her asshole over Hilary's mouth, crying out, "Lick it, bitch," as she continued to finger her own cunt. The soft mounds of the young woman's ass surrounded

The Applicant

Hilary's face, and Hilary lost herself to the strangeness of her new role. She thrust her tongue hard against the tightly puckered little hole and plowed into the narrow, mysterious canal. Liza could see Hilary's tongue get lost in the orifice between the two plump cheeks that pumped up and down, up and down. Hilary used her teeth, as well, to dig deeper into the woman's bottom hole, and then plunged her tongue into the very depth of the anal canal, spreading it wide open while filling it up to the brim.

The recipient of this anal tongue-fuck was nearly delirious with pleasure. "Oh yes, bitch! Yes, keep sucking me," she commanded. "Yeah." The woman rocked back and forth over Hilary's mouth as the younger woman continued to rim her lustily. At last the woman fell hard against Hilary, anchoring herself against the soft body, digging her fingernails into the tender flesh as she rocked with a powerful orgasm.

As soon as the woman had come, the other woman grabbed a double dildo and inserted it into her own cunt and then into Hilary's. The woman began to thrust hard against Hilary's body, and Hilary returned the thrust.

The two-headed rubber cock gave each woman about five or six inches, and they moved into a scissors position so they could maximize the amount of cock they could stuff into their cunts. They had the cock rammed so far in that their cunt-lips were touching, and they were close enough to tongue kiss and suck each other's titties. Then the other woman got real close and practically mounted Hilary's body, bringing their clits kissing-close as well. The woman fucked and pumped and rubbed until she felt her orgasm creeping out of her groin, dripping down her pussy. She panted and groaned as the explosion ripped through her. Hilary picked up the cue and rubbed hard against the woman's twat, taking the rubber cock in far as she could get it and feeling the familiar, welcomed tingle between her legs. Although her body was nearing exhaustion, she felt another orgasm flooding her being. Each thrust of the rubber cock deep inside her body aroused more passion, despite her fatigue, as the other woman continued to take her own pleasure with the tool. Hilary's pleasure seemed to come from a deeper place than she had ever known, and she began to thrust back against the woman and the long dildo inside her cunt. Hilary pushed her body against the limits she'd once given herself out of fear and convention. She moaned in a guttural, primal, untamed expression of lust, and her cries melded with the other woman's equally wild gasps of pleasure. Hilary's body tensed, and she stopped moving. She felt as though she were animated in some distant dimension, and then the older woman fell hard against her, screaming out her own pleasure and giving the dildo one last forceful shove into the younger woman. Hilary's body collapsed, and her mind fell into that strange dimension of absolute elation—and ultimate exhaustion. The room was suddenly very quiet, and *all* the bodies became still.

The sound of a brisk wind could be heard through the high basement window. Somewhere a faucet was dripping, and its muted sound was deafening in the silence. The room was hot from the heat of fucking, but it was waning quickly as the coolness began to eat away at the tepid warmth.

Liza felt the silence. It was like an orgasm had taken her and shaken her very core; and though she had not touched herself, she'd become such a part of the frenzied coupling that her body felt somewhat satisfied by the image the combined bodies had given her.

The Applicant

There was so much that she wanted for Hilary, so many ways of experiencing pleasure. She wanted to give her the opportunity of tasting myriad new desires. She wanted Hilary more than ever because she felt that she'd found the perfect female mate—the epitome of the aggressive submissive with a mind and body to compliment her own.

She longed for the drama to be over, to take Hilary for her own, and for her own pleasure to begin. It had been so different for Liza—her prize had been different at the end of her test. But her test had been one of submission fueled by knowing that on the other side of the drama there were certain desires to be fulfilled. That made the experience complete. Making these desires and fantasies a reality gave the submission meaning; being challenged mentally and physically lifted sexual satisfaction to an almost religious peak.

"Untie her," Liza ordered.

How sweet her four little slaves were, and how well they'd performed their tasks. None of the slaves had been the applicant that Liza had been seeking, but they had intrigued her enough to become lesser instruments of her teaching. None of them had had that special vibrancy and energy that made them rise above the common fuck, nor that unnameable quality that made someone able to be lifted above banality to something rare. The slaves would always be very good—in fact they would always perform better than most lovers; but none was truly extraordinary. When Liza had met Hilary, she had known instantly that she had found special mystery.

"Tie her on the platform, ass wide," Liza ordered.

The slaves knew exactly what their mistress wanted, and as Liza left the room, they were already complying with her demand. In Liza's eyes there was a necessary ruthlessness that she'd learned from Oliver. She felt driven by the darkness and coldness that dwelled within her; it was the force that now drove her slaves and Hilary forward and beyond. There was a kind of animal determination in Liza's features that would have frightened Hilary had she seen it.

As Hilary was pulled from the comfort of the cushion on the floor, she vaguely felt that the climate of the events had changed rather dramatically. She felt that fate was hurtling her toward something ultimately dangerous. All she could do at this point was follow where her mistress led.

CHAPTER VII

Seven

It was time for the first unveiling of her prize. Oliver had recognized Liza's need for a woman, and he had allowed for it under the condition that the woman would also be a source of his own pleasure. The time had come for him to share with Liza the preparation of their charge. It was time for Hilary to be introduced to her master, and it was time for Liza to step aside and prove to Oliver how well she had prepared the young woman.

As Liza climbed the stairs, she could feel herself coming that much closer to the fulfillment that had obsessed her since the inception of the plan. Liza was filled with a sense of the power of her lust. She considered how she had orchestrated every scene, nurtured every little sensual detail, so that both Hilary and Oliver would be seduced and enticed by one another and by Liza herself. Climbing the stairs to retrieve Oliver gave Liza a sense of triumph, for introducing Oliver would set into motion the final acts of Hilary's training, and they would at last be able to enjoy her together.

As Liza reached the top of the stairs, she could hardly contain herself. It had been a strained several weeks with Oliver. He could become so introverted and brooding. When he withdrew into his dark world Liza felt excluded and afraid. Yet she had to admit to herself that she had been rather occupied with thoughts of Hilary and hadn't paid him proper attention. It would be advantageous for them to return to one another.

It didn't occur to her that, in this interim, he would retreat to the warm, wet places he had known before Liza; that he would go back to fucking her archrival. But the cries wafted as she climbed the stairs; the sounds were so loud and so primal that they reached down through the ducts that ran into the cellar. It was a man and a woman making juicy, loud, delicious fuck noises; it was Liza's man and a woman she despised.

The passage to their room was only fifteen feet from the stairs, so it was easy to hear who it was behind the closed door of the bedroom. Her pride was instantly wounded as she realized that Diana and Oliver were fucking lustily behind the door. Fucking in her bed! Liza was seething as she listened to them screaming and growling like rutting animals.

Liza did not know whether to walk in and throw the bitch out of her bed, or whether it would be wiser to turn on her heels and walk away. Diana ... how Liza would love to spit in her face. She wanted nothing more than to slap the woman's face in rage, and

The Applicant

she wanted Oliver to see her venom. But then she knew that he would stand there coldly distant, and Liza would suddenly feel like a petulant child. Worse than these conflicted feelings were the feelings of arousal that were awakening in her body because of the wild, bestial sounds emanating from behind the door. Despite her rage, Liza found herself wishing to join them. She wanted to watch them fucking. At the same time she wanted to run away and cry like a child. But she could not deny the moisture between her legs, or her pussy generating love juice as she listened. She reached between her thighs and touched the wet mound of clean, hot flesh, and she began to finger herself as she listened to her husband fuck another woman. The more furious the sounds from the room, the more furious was Liza's masturbation as she matched her rhythmic caresses to the cadence of Diana's orgasm. Liza pumped her body against the wall, her cunt against her hand as she listened to Oliver coming, his groaning long and deep. Liza's own pleasure cries began to escape her lips as she bucked herself against her sopping wet fingers, an orgasm sweeping over her body. She cried out with intense pleasure.

The bedroom door opened with startling swiftness. Liza was caught with her fingers still lingering on her pussy, and her face reddened with childish shame. He stood at the door looking at her with cool detachment.

"You could've joined us, my love," he said with a calm smile.

"I—I thought I'd let you have your fun," she replied, attempting to match his calm smile.

Oliver chuckled.

"So you got yourself off on our fucking?" quipped Diana. She lay against the pillows on the bed, her wild red hair strewn across the casing, her voluptuous body and lovely porcelain skin set off beautifully against the green sheets.

Liza could not respond to Diana without revealing her fury, so she let the comment go unanswered.

"Hilary is ready for you, my sweet," Liza said, turning to Oliver.

His eyebrows raised in reply. It seemed, from the expression on his face, that he had something more to say.

"Diana dear," Liza said directly to the other woman, "I need to speak with Oliver alone."

Diana smirked and pulled herself out of the bed, draping a silk dressing gown over her naked form. She smiled at Liza and then cast a lusty glance at Oliver and without turning around said, "I see I've trained my little one well."

"Damn her!" Liza screamed when Diana was gone.

"Liza," Oliver said with an ironic grin on his lips, "your jealousy is so charming." He kissed her on the forehead.

"I hate her."

"You simply hate the part of her that resembles yourself," he replied. He went to the couch and picked up his jeans and shirt.

Liza realized that she couldn't say more without damning herself to possible tortures she didn't want to endure. Clearly, Oliver was getting her back for fucking the young stud Stephen in their marital bed. And besides, Oliver had a passion for Diana, just as Liza had her passion for Stephen. They allowed each other their separate affairs.

"Besides, my dear," he said as he laced up his boots, "you love who she's been and still is to you, whether you want to admit it or not."

The Applicant

Liza seethed inwardly, knowing that Oliver was right, and his knowledge of her made her angry. But she was grateful to Oliver, and she hated to admit it but she was also grateful to Diana for bringing her and Oliver together.

She watched him as he finished dressing. He was such an alluring man, and Liza found herself wanting him right at that moment. She wanted to stop everything and have him all to herself for many long hours. To hell with everything else: Hilary, the cellar, the slaves, Diana and Stephen. All she wanted now was for Oliver to take charge of her body, take charge of her being and use her as he wished. She wanted to give herself to him as no other woman ever had or ever would. She wanted to bend over and offer her ass to her husband, to give him the tight orifice of love he so coveted and allow him to plunge himself into the depths of her, lost in his obsession with anal loving.

Her body was vibrating, exuding the force of her desires. Oliver looked at Liza and recognized the passion and returned the energy. He knew exactly what she wanted, and he could read the lust in her eye and the intention in her heart.

"Not now, Liza," he said. His amusement suddenly ran cool. His face was hard, and he was focusing on other intentions now.

She sighed, knowing that, once again, she would have to wait.

"Liza," he spoke sharply.

"Yes, sir," she responded, automatically his submissive.

"I trust that she is ready, because if she's not, you know who will ultimately pay the price?"

"I do not expect her to let you down, sir." She kept her eyes down, displaying her own good training.

She opened the door for her master and followed him out and down to the cellar.

It seemed like hours that Hilary was tied on her hands and knees. Her body was fast reaching the point of exhaustion. She did not know how much more she could take, especially if her captors were without compassion. She was tied over a small bench or stool so that her lower chest and belly were supported. There was a place on the apparatus for her head to rest, though her arms were awkwardly tied and her knees parted so wide that it was almost painful. She was stretched and tied so that her ass was obviously displayed, and the weight of her body not hers to bear.

She sensed that the time had come for the final violation of the last part of her body that had not been used—the part of her body that had been studiously avoided in all her encounters. She was certain about what was to follow, and she was frightened. As she heard voices from the top of the stairs, her body went rigid with terror.

They were like royalty entering. They walked in, the aura of authority preceding them. Liza wore flowing silks that swirled around her as she walked, fabric so sheer that her naked body was clearly visible underneath. Oliver followed, bringing with him a dark persona that was complimented by the light emanating from Liza's being. His was a darkness not of cruelty but the darkness of authority and mystery that keeps his submissive questioning and alive with wonder.

Time seemed to stop in the dank cellar as he entered. It seemed as though expectancy entered with him. Nobody moved including Hilary, who sensed that at last Oliver had come.

Hilary was the target of his intense focus. Her

The Applicant

creamy ass was ripe and open, her anus a little bud in between a mound of tight flesh. He let her feel the stillness and tension in the room, and then he walked toward her and rudely slapped the flesh of her buttocks. Hilary jerked and a small cry escaped her lips. He grabbed a dildo from a table. It was not overly long, only about five inches in length, but it was two full inches in diameter. The others watched him intently as he first caressed her ass, then slapped her hard again. Then he rubbed the dildo up and down the splayed crack of her bottom. After some prolonged teasing, Oliver swiftly lathered her ass with white grease and, with no ceremony, roughly shoved the dildo in her anus.

"NO!" she screamed.

As soon as the word escaped her lips, she regretted it. Her voice shot through the air and hung like a terrible mistake. Her body was still feeling the acute pain of the dildo, and she could not prevent herself from letting the tears well up in her eyes. She could not retract that utterance, even if she could hide her tears behind the blindfold.

Oliver pulled Hilary's head back by her hair. His anger was controlled and focused. She understood his power.

"What did you say?"

His voice chilled her through the marrow.

"I'm sorry, sir," she replied, ashamed.

"Bitch," he sneered. "You'll have to prove your remorse with silence." And with a decisive gesture he grabbed a leather strap from the table and quickly inflicted a dozen blows across her ass.

It took every last ounce of her concentration to keep her from crying out, but she did endure. It seemed that the pain was in every part of her body, and she wanted to scream, as though crying out would ward off the agony. But she wanted her mistress more than she wanted to scream, and so Hilary endured.

"You'd better not be wasting my time," he said bluntly.

His words were a threat to both Hilary and Liza, making the promise of authentic submission more viable than ever. Through his words, Hilary realized that Liza's attentions were a true prize which would not be easily won.

Oliver turned on his heel and left the cellar. Liza followed him. She was slightly afraid, for she was never sure exactly what was on his mind. She never knew when his coldness was sincere or ironic. In their initial plan, Oliver had reserved the right to dismiss Hilary at any given time, and Liza was fearful that he might do just that.

All who were left in the cellar were stunned by his brief presence and waited in frozen silence before anyone had the courage to move.

Morning dawned brightly in the room where Hilary slept. She'd been carried there, though she hardly remembered. She suspected she was in the same room where she had first been taken at the beginning of this arduous weekend. Beyond the blindfold, Hilary could sense that the room was light and airy. She felt the warmth of the sun on her naked back, and she could feel the soft texture of the silky fabrics of the pillows against her body. The smell of coffee wafted through the room. She knew instinctively that there would be no more adventures for the weekend, and the thought saddened her.

"Get up," a male voice commanded her.

She rose to her feet, unbalanced and unused to navigating under her own power. No hands came to her aid, except a single pair that guided her to a

The Applicant

warm, soapy bath where she was washed in a perfunctory way. There was no sensual play, there were no caressing hands to soothe her alienation. And then before she knew it, she was once again seated on a low stool with her wrists bound behind her, her pussy and breasts exposed. She sat waiting, wondering if this torment would go on for hours as it had previously. But rather suddenly, her blindfold was stripped from her eyes, and she closed them, shielding herself from the flood of white light that blinded her. Soon her eyes began to adjust, and she found that she was seated in the morning room. She gazed at Stephen and Liza as they stood before her in exactly the same positions they had been in on Friday.

"Untie her," Liza instructed Stephen. Her voice was devoid of any emotion.

Hilary had hoped that her mistress would at last give her the attentions she craved so desperately. But Liza's gaze was icy and dictatorial.

Liza stared at Hilary's beautiful body. Behind the mask of detachment, her fires burned more passionately than ever for the young woman.

"Crawl to me," Liza ordered.

Hilary slowly raised herself from the stool and moved onto the floor, crouching on all fours. She took great pleasure in humbling herself before her mistress as she crawled to her.

"You're fortunate that you are still allowed in this house. Your outburst in front of your master is a transgression."

"I'm sorry."

"You realize that Oliver was rather lenient with you?"

"Yes." Hilary kept her head bowed.

"Such behavior will not be tolerated again. If you

transgress again your removal will be swift and certain. Is that understood?"

"Yes."

"Good."

And then it seemed to Hilary that Liza's tone softened almost imperceptibly.

"This is for you," she said, as she held out a small package. "Your things are waiting for you at the door. You will return to this house only when you are summoned."

"Then I will not be coming Friday night?"

"You will return to this house only when you are summoned," Liza repeated coldly.

Hilary rose from her place before her mistress, and keeping her eyes down, made her way to the door. She quickly collected her personal belongings and silently left.

CHAPTER VIII

Eight

Life at the estate with Oliver and Liza was a secret existence, but it had become so intrusive in her other world that Hilary was no longer certain which reality was more plausible to her. Home and work seemed bland and ordinary, as if she was going through the motions of an old habit; her activities held little meaning for her. She craved to be back in the world of Liza and Oliver and unbridled, submissive lust. Her cunt oozed just thinking about it.

"This belongs in your ass," read the note Hilary found in the package Liza sent her home with.

The message was significantly precise.

Also in the package was a dildo—the same one that Oliver had rammed up her ass.

"Use it now. Use it everyday. Don't disappoint me."

The last thing in the world Hilary wanted to do was let Liza down. She loved her and wanted her. She wanted her body, her tongue, her hands, her reciprocated love. Hilary wanted everything that Liza represented. She wanted to bathe in the fire of her wild sexual presence; she wanted to be next to the woman who was the catalyst that was igniting passions dark and light within her. The dark had become so seductive, and Hilary knew that at the estate she would be allowed to explore those fantasies.

She wore the dildo in her ass during the evening when she returned from work. Each evening she would bend before her mirror, spread the cheeks of her bare ass, rub a lubricant into the tight orifice and insert the fat dildo into her contracting opening. It was the second of many intrusions into her other life, the first being the collar that she had not removed from her neck all that weekend. The collar and the dildo were strong reminders of the estate and the glaring difference between her two worlds.

Yet life with the collar, dildo, and fantasies was becoming an integral part of her being, intrusive as they were. She came to enjoy them, as she did the third intrusion, which was the lavender envelopes that appeared each morning; they were pushed under her door during the night. It gave her a curious thrill to know that someone stalked her hall at night and left the messages for her. Did this mysterious delivery person know the contents of the envelopes?

On Monday morning the first message read:
DO NOT REMOVE THE COLLAR ALL DAY.

Hilary didn't mind. In fact, she didn't want to take the collar off for it was by now a welcome restraint around her neck, and it made her cunt throb when she wore it tight. She had never ventured to wear it to work, and the thought of mixing the two worlds

The Applicant

made her thrill with the danger of being discovered and exposed. She couldn't help wondering what people in the workday world would think of her bizarre accessory, but she was more concerned about disappointing her mistress, and more still, was worried about the punishment she would receive for disobedience.

It took her a few hours in the morning to get used to her image in the mirror. She selected a dress that would set the collar off as though it were a piece of unusual jewelry. She decided that it didn't look too bold or obvious, and so she walked out her apartment with an air of secret confidence.

Throughout the day she wondered if it was stares of admiration or knowing or simple curiosity that the collar attracted. At times she wondered if it wasn't merely her self-consciousness that made it seem as though she were attracting more attention, her nervousness presuming the stares of curiosity. The other side of her emotions was cluttered with feelings of intense arousal that were clear and definite. Her body was nearly at a peak all day. Hilary was ready for sex as she sat squirming on her stool, frustrated at the long hours that ticked by too slowly.

Tuesday morning there was the second lavender envelope with the exotic purple ink.

WEAR THE DILDO ALL DAY.

Her body cringed at the lewd idea, and simultaneously she welcomed the thought.

As she wore the reminder, hidden deep within her anus, there was not a minute of the day that she was not conscious of her separate life. She enjoyed the discomfort of being impaled by the thick plastic member while she sat enacting business transactions. The dildo seemed to work its way more deeply into her ass as she sat there; each time she moved, the dildo inched further up inside her. Wearing the dildo in place all day was an act of submission that pleased her and kept her body on the edge of climax all day long.

At five o'clock she began to close her desk and was preparing to leave when there was a phone call for her.

It was a woman's voice.

"Walk to 12th Street and in the department store on the southwest corner and find the ladies room in the women's apparel department. In the first bathroom stall, exchange the clothes you are wearing for the ones hanging on the back of the door there." And then she hung up.

Hilary was shocked and afraid. She had no idea what they intended for her to do, but she sensed that it was something outrageous or dangerous. She could feel her heart beating rapidly, and her breath seemed to almost materialize in front of her as she panted with anxiety and excitement. She was diving into a vast unknown in playing these games with Liza, Oliver, and the others. They were veritable strangers, yet Hilary was obliged to trust them completely; and she was far too involved to stop now.

Hilary knew the store that the woman had mentioned on the phone, and she walked the ten blocks to it as though in a dream. She made her way to the ladies room and pulled at the door with some hesitation. Once she was on the other side of that door she wouldn't be able to turn back. For a split second Hilary wanted to turn and run away. All of a sudden all her old fears and conventional emotions flooded her being, attempting to make her stop; her old self was trying to force the newer emerging self to return to safety and abort the whole adventure. Her loins burned, and with determination she pulled the door open, plunging herself forward into the unknown.

The Applicant

The clothes were waiting in the stall for her. She grabbed the hanger quickly to keep herself from backing out of her commitment. The clothes were unlike anything she had ever owned or worn. There were bright red spandex stretch pants and a spandex top that was cut so low in the front that her cleavage and her hardened nipples were apparent to any eye. There was a silver belt to tie around her waist and five-inch spike heels that fit her perfectly.

As she emerged from the stall, she looked at herself in the mirror and realized that she had been ordered to dress like a tease, a slut. She'd looked that way at the estate before, but never in her "other life." The clothes hugged Hilary's body so closely that not one curve, not one voluptuous crevice, went unseen. She wondered if she would attract lewd stares, and if other women would notice as she knew that men would. She wondered if she would win some propositions dressed so much like a whore. For Hilary, it would be a daring act to merely step out of the ladies room. But at last she did just that, and she made her way out of the department store and down onto the street.

It was a little past five, and the street was crowded with people on their way home from work. Most were walking hurriedly with their faces cast down, simply concentrating on getting home. Yet Hilary did not go unnoticed.

At first she felt extremely self-conscious, but as she began to notice that men, and even some women, were looking at her with some interest, she thrust out her breasts and strutted down the street, acting the part that her outfit demanded. She wanted them to look at her, and as she walked down the street, her desire began to burn beneath her flesh. She began to enjoy the attention, realizing that she had thought and dreamed of strangers desiring her as they were while she moved down the street, but she had always been afraid to explore her own exhibitionistic instincts on her own. Now she had Liza to guide her, and Hilary would do anything for Liza. She began to feel the dampness in her crotch and thought of the sexual power taking her over. At last she found her car and slipped inside.

As she drove home, she could not keep herself from reaching between her legs with one hand. She couldn't stop her needs from being satisfied, and as she drove out onto the expressway, her fingers explored her wet pussy. She spread her legs as wide as she possibly could and opened the plump lips of her cunt so that she could caress her burning flesh more easily as she drove. She didn't care that truckers who passed her could see her playing with herself; in fact, she wanted to expose herself to their hungry eyes. Her fingers rubbed and teased her pussy furiously, the sweet wetness of her cunt was flowing freely over her fingers. Her pleasure was enhanced by the dildo still shoved deeply into her asshole. As Hilary pumped against her own fingers, her asshole tightened itself against the dildo. The instrument expanded everything inside her, opening her to deeper pleasures. Her orgasm nearly began to spill; she forced herself to stop the beautiful waves of pleasure that made her body move and buck and shudder from her shoulders to her toes. Her pleasure was wild and free, enhanced by her moving vehicle but she could not allow the ultimate pleasure of coming; she could not cheat on her mistress. Her pussy could not come by her own hand unless Liza was there to watch. She was grateful that there was little traffic so that she could speed her car along, matching its velocity with the force of her pleasure.

The Applicant

When she arrived home, she entered her apartment in a daze. She went to the bathroom and looked at herself in the mirror and was amazed at her reflection; she was also amazed at her own boldness. There was a beauty in what she saw, and it was as if she hardly recognized herself; there was a dark mystery in her eyes that excited and frightened her.

Later that evening, before she retired to bed, another envelope was slid under her door. She paused as she saw it in the hallway. Her body began to churn as if on cue. She felt apprehension, fear, and ultimately a curiosity that took control of her loins. She thirsted for something she had never known. She realized after the events of the day that she had just began to uncover the possibilities of her own sexuality.

She played cat and mouse with the envelope, and it seemed to call to her. She let her body simmer with the expectation and let it sit for twenty minutes before she went to pick it up. Fear had also kept her from picking it up, but at last curiosity prevailed, and she anxiously tore open the lavender envelope.

YOU'RE BECOMING THE PERFECT WHORE. DON'T STOP.

Curiously, she appreciated the sound of the word "whore." It jolted her and radically altered her own perception of herself. She was also surprised to realize that someone had witnessed her performance. She had had no idea. Who could could it have been? Stephen? Liza? Oliver? Or perhaps it was someone that she had yet to meet. She fell asleep wondering, a smile of satisfaction crossing her face; she was appreciated.

Wednesday morning she dashed for her front door, expecting to find an envelope, and was utterly disappointed to find nothing. She felt lost without instructions for her day. She had grown used to the challenges; she wanted them, and without the lewd instructions Hilary felt alone. The thirst she had known for those secret delights had not been quenched.

CHAPTER IX

Nine

"So what are your plans for the little tart today?" Stephen asked.

"Whatever she likes," Liza replied.

"We're not going to jerk her chain today?"

"No new envelopes. I am letting her store her energy because soon 'her chain' is going to be yanked very hard indeed."

Stephen laughed, completely understanding his mistress.

"She's ripe for it," he sneered.

"I haven't even begun to make her sweat," Liza said.

"You're very good at this," Stephen observed, as he sat across from her in a lounge chair. He was dressed in his usual casual attire: T-shirt, jeans and boots. Liza had called him to her room that morning, her fires burning and her body ready for a good, hard fuck, and her sweet Oliver away on business. She lounged in her robe, her breasts falling free from the fabric, her cunt visible as she allowed the sun to play on her beautiful body.

Stephen slouched in the chair and gazed at her, eyeing her shaved pussy and its pouting lips, hungrily. He loved watching her, loved the way she moved so comfortably in her nudity and the way she arched her eyebrows when she spoke in a coy manner. He liked the way her half-clothed body kept him anxious, kept him wondering when she might leap up and fling her garment away and attack him, taking his aching cock in her mouth and sucking him in, tasting him deeply. He imagined getting fed up with her sassiness, and in his mind's eye he saw himself rising and ripping the robe off her, simply claiming his treasure, rather than waiting for his treasure to claim him.

He loved watching her as much as she loved being watched. Sometimes, Liza would perform quite lewdly for him. Once she danced for him for a full hour, with no rest, moving and undulating around him using scarves, feathers, and leather straps. She pressed her tits, her pussy, and her ass against his face and body in a tantalizing, teasing way and rubbed up against his hard cock until he was clearly aching with desire. Her pussy was flowing from all the excitement and her body was exhausted, but just as she was ready to mount him and take his hardness deep into the soft, dark, wet chamber of her desire, he changed the rules and the roles: He took charge and wouldn't let her stop dancing and grinding against him until *he* was ready to take her. He was attempting to separate Liza from her pleasure so that he could successfully

The Applicant

steal from her. He wanted to take control of her, take away her power and her ability to create her own pleasure. But Liza could not be separated from her pleasure—not by Stephen anyway. Her body became electrified if she was servicing someone else's desires, as well as if someone was concentrating only on her pleasure. She had made the dance like the actual act of fucking, and as Stephen watched, she rubbed her cunt in a hundred ways, each without the touch of her hand. Stephen's little power play excited them both, and the two of them created enough heat to launch a space shuttle, just by generating intense sexual energy. As Liza danced and created friction between her legs, Stephen's cock became an accessory to her dance, one she'd tease and taunt as she moved. Soon, the two of them were shooting wild spasms of come, exploding without having fucked. Then, when the last bit of orgasm rocked through them, they fucked like wild animals in heat. Stephen tossed Liza on the floor, spread her wide open and plunged in his still-hard cock, going deep on the very first thrust. She received him, opening totally and pushing herself up to greet his thrusts. The excitement of the hard, tantalized cock gliding into the creamy, warm cunt sent them both into another orgasmic frenzy. They came—loudly, with much commotion. Then they separated and fell back on the floor with a sigh.

"Of course I am good at what I do," rejoined Liza.

"Yes, that's because you're a bitch."

"I'd love to do the same to you someday. I'd love to watch you squirm and suffer underneath me, begging me for more," she taunted him.

"You're tempting me again, you bitch," he said, the anger and frustration rising in his voice.

"You are astute, dear Stephen," she replied as she lay on her bed. Her robe had fallen open, completely revealing her body.

"I want you now," he said huskily, moving toward her on the bed.

"No," she said cattily.

"Are you trying to piss me off?" he growled.

"Perhaps," she hissed.

She could feel his anger begin to rise from deep within him. She was enjoying manipulating him as much as he was enjoying being toyed with. He wanted to attack her, hold her down and punish her for trying to unman him. He wanted nothing more than to pound himself into her hard and furiously, taking her cunt, her mouth, her asshole. He wanted to fuck her so hard that it was brutal. But Stephen held back, for taking her in the heat of anger was off limits. She was allowed to taunt him, but he would be disobeying if he responded, especially if he responded physically. Knowing these limits made him burn all the more furiously, his anger growing rich and wild inside his mind and in between his thighs. Suddenly his anger broke through his restraint.

"I don't care about the rules anymore, you bitch. I am going to take you now," he said.

She thrilled with dangerous excitement. She wanted him to take her with his anger billowing almost out of control. She wanted him to dominate her at last, and that domination would take force, perhaps even violence. The time had come, and Liza was ready, though she knew she was breaking a cardinal rule: Oliver was not there. And she was alone with Stephen and his wrath.

Stephen could feel the darkness rising within him, and the possibility of finally taking her as he pleased was rapidly becoming a probability. It seemed as if

The Applicant

the two of them were moving through a dream that had been rehearsed over and over in their imaginations. He stood up from his place on the lounge. Pictures of humiliating her, fucking her, forcing her to grovel and moan under his body flashed through his mind.

"Stop!" A voice pierced through their fantasy world.

Stephen kept moving toward Liza.

"Stop!" the voice roared again.

Suddenly reality caught Stephen, and he felt discomfort rise in his throat.

"Get out, Stephen."

Stephen froze.

Like a Cheshire cat, Liza lured him, beckoned him toward the bed.

But his better judgement took over, and Stephen backed off. Then it became clear who had cracked the code of their fantasy and interrupted their animal instincts. Oliver stood in the corner of the room, and he moved forward to stand between the bed and Stephen. His dark eyes peered deeply into Stephen's. Oliver's expression was not angry or cruel. His eyes were calm and stoney.

"Now is not the time."

Stephen realized that Oliver was right, and he forced his passions to cool. As soon as he completely came out of his fierce fantasy state, Stephen realized that he was standing only inches from Oliver's face.

As Liza watched them, she could almost feel her pussy dripping with come, so exciting did she find the scene before her. To her it was like watching warriors, two armed men square off for battle; and she was the prize. She watched their pulsing bodies nearly glow with predatory tension, and she realized that any moment the game could turn on her, making her the focus of their anger. She let out her breath as she watched Stephen turn and silently leave the room.

Oliver still stood with his back to the bed. He remained that way for too long, and Liza began to get nervous. Suddenly he turned. His voice was utterly cold and quiet.

"Don't ever do that again." Though he spoke the words quietly, they seemed to pin Liza back to the sheets with their power.

"What do you mean?" she said quickly. "It was wonderful...."

"It was dangerous," he cut her off. "And incredibly stupid. You could've been hurt."

Liza was stunned. It was not like Oliver to lace his words with such vehement cold. She felt like a child being scolded and blistered by his lashing tongue. It could not have hurt more had he paddled her butt till it was raw, and there was something in his demeanor that hinted that he was not too far off from doing precisely that.

"If you want to play with that man's rage, if you want to entice him to rape you, I won't try to stop it. But how dare you try anything while I'm not here."

He was very angry, but he was in total control of his rage, unlike Stephen. Oliver could step into any situation and command every action and every player. Liza was awed by his authority over her, and she was captivated by his self-control. She sat up in the bed, her silk robe falling away. She was waiting for his further command or punishment. But he said nothing; he did not respond to her desire. Instead, he continued to pierce her being with his icy stare.

"Don't leave this room today."

"But Oliver, I've things to do...."

He was at the door and ready to depart when her

The Applicant

words gushed out to stop him. He turned and gave her a steely glare.

"Don't leave this room until I come and get you. Have I made myself clear?"

"Yes, sir," she replied, subdued.

He walked out of the room, closing the door firmly behind him. Liza heard the key in her lock, and the sound clearly sealed her fate.

The next morning there was still no envelope. There were no phone calls to reassure her. There had been nothing to link Hilary with Liza or Oliver except the collar, the dildo, the clothing, and her vivid memories; yet with each day, those memories became more distant, further removed from "real life." There was no predetermined date for her return, and she wondered if she would be invited back at all. The thought of not ever returning filled Hilary with a kind of desperate panic. Were they no longer interested in her? Or had she failed to perform in some intrinsic way? She considered every dire possibility, and her instinct told her finally that the adventure was not over. But the deep knowledge of this did not keep her from wondering and worrying whether she was performing as a compliant and proper submissive. She wanted nothing more than to please her master and, of course, her mistress.

Liza's feelings during her first twenty-four hours of imprisonment vacillated between rage and bewilderment. Oliver had never been so angry with her, and he'd never stayed mad for so long. She had expected him to return during the night, yet he had not come. She had no food until morning. The maid had come early and left her a tray without waking her.

She had no way to appeal her fate and she knew

that Oliver would not come to her until he was ready. And that could be a long time. Liza began to panic, worrying about the party, the weekend. And she worried about Hilary. It was bad enough that she could not communicate with her charge; it must be horrible for Hilary.

It was Friday morning and again there were no envelopes; the phone remained conspicuously quiet. Hilary's heart sank. She removed the collar she'd been wearing all night and the dildo she'd worn as well. She placed the items carefully in the little leather bag that she kept them in and went to work without them.

There was no breakfast tray in Liza's room Friday morning. She bolted from her bed and raced for the door. It was unlocked, and that fact startled her. She was uncertain about what to do. Did she dare leave and violate Oliver's orders? Or was the open door a sign that she was free to leave?

Unable to contain herself, Liza chose to see the unlocked door as a sign of her freedom. After all, it was Friday. Not any Friday, but the beginning of a long weekend that Liza had spent much time planning for. She made her way down to the kitchen.

"Laura, where's Oliver?" she asked the maid as she entered the warm kitchen. The aroma of breakfast filled her nostrils.

"I saw him in the garden about an hour ago."

"Thank you," she replied, and she dashed out the door and down the steps, wearing nothing more than a white T-shirt. She ran through the grass, reveling in her freedom. She ran behind the stable and found Oliver tending some plants. He looked up and watched her tentatively approach him.

The Applicant

"I'm sorry," she stammered, feeling as though she had interrupted a sacred moment. Apologizing seemed the only appropriate way she could begin speaking to him.

"I doubt that," he replied, and continued to tend the rosebushes.

"No, I am. I truly am sorry. Forgive me."

"There is nothing to forgive."

"You want to watch me suffer, don't you?" Her anger was rising, while he remained calm, with a bemused smile slowly crossing his lips.

He stopped his gardening and looked at her thoughtfully.

"I hope you've been through hell these last two days. If you haven't learned your lesson, I'll lock you up for another two days." He was completely serious, but he was no longer angry.

She wanted to resume their relationship without the anger, and it was obvious that that wouldn't happen until she had been dangled before him, until he had taken all the satisfaction he wanted from watching her writhe.

"Yes, sir," she said.

He dropped his spade in the dirt and walked toward her until they stood face to face. He maintained the same steely visage. She shivered as she ventured to look into his black eyes.

"There is one thing that you need to understand from your silly escapades. You took a terrible risk in inciting Stephen to anger. He can be more cruel and frightening than even you can imagine. For his sake and for yours, it was foolish of you to manipulate him the way you did without me here. If you try it again, I shall fire him, and I'll unleash such a punishment upon you, you will most certainly never try anything like it again. Do you understand?" There seemed to be a spark of fire rising in his eyes.

Tears began to well in Liza's eyes as her gaze met his. Once again she felt like a sheepish child who was being castigated. She loved Oliver more than ever because, once again, he proved himself to be her master. She realized how much she truly needed him. She knew that he loved her to the core—even the side of her that disobeyed and was often wildly out of control. But she knew that Oliver was her safety net in the wonderful world of sexual adventures they were creating at the estate. Her sexuality was reckless without his distance and restraint. Because Oliver loved her, he would never let her go too far; he would never let her fall too deeply into something if he feared that she might not come out unharmed. Her union with Oliver was a perfect match of light and dark, and while she was the creator that kept their relationship bold and new and vital, Oliver was the one that kept them safe.

That thought was the source of her tears. A single droplet strayed down her cheek as she was reminded of their love, as she realized how serious he was and how acute his judgment was. She was suddenly overwhelmed by the passion of his protectiveness. He placed no limits on her desires—he requested only that he be present for their execution. She thought at once about Stephen, and she realized that perhaps she didn't have the insight to judge him beyond the facets of his personality that she found charming. Perhaps it took someone with Oliver's dark nature to understand another with darker passions.

"I'm sorry, Oliver." It was all she could manage to say.

At last a smile crossed his lips, making his face instantly warm and beautiful.

The Applicant

"You have a full day ahead of you. Our guests begin arriving in two hours. I'd suggest that you start to get ready."

He watched her as she smiled and dashed back up toward the house. He chuckled as he watched her lovely body in motion, her beautiful ass exposed in the morning light.

As Liza disappeared into the house, Oliver left the garden and entered the stable. He went up the stairs to the apartment where Stephen lived. He opened the door and said, "I must speak with you, Stephen."

Hilary sat at her teller's window, preoccupied with her depression. At one o'clock the supervisor came to her and said, "You have a phone call. Why don't you take your lunch now."

Hilary locked up quickly and grabbed the phone in an empty office.

"Hilary," the voice said in a cool, calm, yet commanding tone. It was Liza.

Hilary's heart raced at once. Her body tingled immediately to the familiar feel of sexual energy fluttering through her loins, up and down her spine.

"I—I ..." she stammered. "Yes," she finally said.

"I've startled you."

"Yes. I didn't expect you to call."

"Oliver wishes to see you. I need you at the estate at seven. Wear the attire I've provided you with. And of course you must wear the collar and the dildo."

"Understood."

Liza hung up, leaving Hilary so shaken that she had to sit down for a moment.

She felt like a puppet, jerked around with strings by unseen hands. It never occurred to here that she would not comply with her mistress' orders. The soft sounds of Liza's voice lured her again, to the possibility of melting into that delicious body at long last. And Oliver. It seemed strange that he had requested her presence. Her body began to pulse, and she realized that she would have to take the rest of the day off. She knew that she was going to be useless at work: Her mind was totally fixated on the adventures that awaited her that evening at the estate. Hilary left the office to tell her supervisor that she had to leave. There was an emergency, she claimed.

She smiled to herself: a sexual emergency that required immediate attention. Her pussy and asshole tingled with anticipatory excitement and pleasure. She could physically feel her fantasies in motion, and as she headed home she could swear it was Liza's mouth working deliciously on her cunt, sucking vigorously on her swelled and aching clitoris. She came as she pulled out of her parking space at work and headed home. She could swear it was Liza's mouth.

CHAPTER X

Ten

Liza hung up the phone. Her last call had been made. Her guests were already arriving and it was time for her to go out and join them. She quickly dressed in red lace panties and a black robe. She didn't bother with shoes, as she calmly walked out to the pool to meet her guests. They were all there, and she had at one time or another known each and every one of them intimately. She knew their bodies well—by choice or command she'd fucked them all, both women and men. There were ten gathered, plus Diana and Stephen, if he chose to join them, for he had been invited to join in the games that were planned for the weekend. Including herself, Oliver, and Hilary, there were fifteen—a perfect number for a weekend of delight.

"My dear, you look charming," Diana gushed. "Not too pale from your forced bed rest, I see."

Liza was taken aback that Diana knew about her punishment, and she wondered if any of the others were aware of her shameful reprimand. She quickly walked away from the brazen bitch and went to greet the rest of her guests.

Liza approached her friends and lovers with hugs and passionate kisses, and they in turn warmed her with smiles and affectionate pats on all the right places. Her infectious sensuality was intoxicating, and she was buoyed by their attentiveness. She was pleased to be the center of so much sexual attention, the centerpiece, the seductress of her own estate. She was the catalyst that had lured them all there, and she was clearly pleased with her accomplishments.

"I understand you have a little tidbit we're all going to get a chance to taste?" said a gorgeous, blue-eyed, blonde woman.

Liza smiled.

"It's been a long time, Stella. I'm so pleased that you could come."

"I can't forget two years ago. I had the most delightful sex I've ever had with you and Oliver. I expect this weekend will be no less, since I know it's you running the show this time."

"Oliver is as much the master as he ever was."

"Oh," smiled Stella, "but now he's in love, and that makes all difference."

Liza smiled broadly within herself. She was pleased that everyone here recognized what she'd become in Oliver's life. This knowledge satisfied her deeply. She was filled with the great excitement of the unknown, for her guests were going to experience something they'd never known at the estate before.

The Applicant

"Liza, you're looking lovely," said Adam, a tall, dark-haired Adonis-type whose tanned body was delicious to look at, yet whose personality left much to be desired. His hand was already placed firmly on her bare ass as he spoke. "You are going to let me have my way with you tonight, aren't you?'

"Oh, we have many things planned," she said with a wink, and she pulled away from him. "Why don't you enjoy the pool. Laura should be here with more drinks shortly."

A few of the guests were already swimming, as others lounged in the warm sun. It was a delectable afternoon, with tastes and smells and caresses that vibrated the ethers around them. There was a certain electricity in the air as a distant summer storm crackled in the far-off horizon.

Liza lay down next to Nancy on a chaise longue. Nancy had been at the estate two years ago. She was a particular favorite of Liza's, not only as a sexual partner but as a friend. She had her own submissive relationship with her husband Joseph, a man whom Liza abhorred. He had a taste for inelegant cruelty, and Liza was grateful that he was unable to attend this weekend. She was pleased to have Nancy's attentions all to herself.

The sun backed down upon her bottom, as she lay in Nancy's arms, allowing the other woman to caress and fondle her as she wished. It felt good to recline for a moment, to take some time to forget the anxious rumblings that had consumed her for the past week. It was a welcome intermission between acts, wherein she could clear her mind and think, a time to repair her injured consciousness and concentrate on thoughts of Hilary.

"Liza."

She opened her eyes, but the sun being too bright to clearly see him. Still she knew his voice.

"Hello Stephen." She rose to face him, rolling over on her side. He sat in a chair leaning toward her. He was the one piece in her intricate puzzle that had not yet fallen into place. For some reason his intrusion irritated her, and his naked torso ignited fires throughout her body.

"What are you doing here?" she asked curtly.

"I've been invited."

Of course he really needed no invitation, but Liza felt at a loss for words, distracted by his body. He was exuding a kind of animal danger that always made her wet.

"Well, I suppose you're all ready for the weekend's festivities?" she said.

"I suppose I am. Are *you*?" he replied, cocking his head to the side.

"A little short on planning time."

She sensed his darker side brewing just below the surface of his civility, and she felt it was as though he were picking up right where they had left off two days before.

"What do you want?" she asked irritably, for now was not the time for their own little psychodrama.

"A little peace of mind."

"Oh *really*?"

Their voices were kept to a low whisper, but the urgent hissing that was passing between them was not going unnoticed.

"You started something on Wednesday...." he said.

"Well now is not the time to finish...."

She resisted the urge to taunt him, though it seemed he was intent on taunting her.

"Don't tempt me, please," she was more serious in her request, fearing that his seduction might work.

The Applicant

He smiled as though he were willing to let the tension diffuse.

"How about a swim?" he asked.

She rose without a second thought, thinking a cool swim would be just the remedy to turn down the volume on the raging fires within them.

Hours passed, and Liza swam and sunbathed with the others. Slowly she began to feel completely restored. Even Stephen was loose and lively with the guests. Liza noticed that he was successfully charming many of the women present.

Liza gazed contentedly around the pool. She watched the beauty of the naked bodies that lounged and swam and occasionally stole little nibbles here and there, unable to avoid the anticipation of more to come. Of all the luscious bodies available to her, Stephen's was the one she desired the most. She watched as Stella and he lightly engaging in a little game of foreplay, and she couldn't resist the temptation to break up their fun.

"Stephen, dear," she spoke abruptly.

He looked up at her, his hand still stroking Stella's thigh, as the woman returned the touch, stroking Stephen's beautiful chest.

"I need to talk to you."

"No you don't." He turned his attention back to Stella.

"Stephen, it's time to get the things ready for the dinner."

"When I'm ready."

He was far from his usual compliant self, for never had Stephen deliberately defied her wishes. Suddenly Liza found herself struggling to retain her position.

"If you don't mind, Stella, Stephen has other things to do. After all, he is under our employ."

"You stay here," Stephen whispered to Stella. "I'll be right back."

Stephen rose and led Liza to a spot away from the pool, under the shade of an enormous maple tree.

"I don't appreciate your playing little trump cards while I'm engrossed in other matters. Or is that just your jealousy showing?"

"I don't understand what you're trying to do, but you do work here and you have a job you are being paid to do. Fucking is merely a side benefit."

"Oh, is that so? Sometimes I feel as though I'm really simply your paid fuck."

"How can you say that?" she nearly shouted. Their voices were growing too intense to go unheard. "I don't know what this is all about, but I'll not have it!"

"Don't you try to manipulate me, you bitch!" He flared back.

"I told you this is not the time," her words were as icy as she could manage. She had never been so cold to him before, and her fury was matching his.

"Oh, you are so wrong. Now *is* the time." The fire was back, blazing as fiercely as it had in the bedroom. It was a fire that she had learned to fear. She turned to look for Oliver, but he was nowhere to be seen. Liza turned her back to go, but Stephen grabbed her wrist and held it tightly. "You aren't going anywhere." He was growling.

By that time all eyes were on them, their words and passion far too loud to go unheeded. It seemed that the day's activities were beginning rather early and there was no one who would dare interrupt.

"Oliver ..." she hissed into Stephen's face.

"Fuck Oliver."

Stephen turned to the group by the pool and saw they were watching with great interest. He continued

The Applicant

to detain Liza with his iron grip. The sneer and gleam that emanated from his eyes and mouth were colored with evil.

"Your hostess has just been reprieved from her forced punishment of two days lockup with only bread and water." His nostrils flared with victory as he mocked her with every word he spoke.

"Stop it!" she seethed through her teeth. "You're overstepping your bounds."

"I don't have any."

"I have Oliver to back me up. I can have you off this estate faster than you know."

Stephen merely scoffed at her assumption. His laugh was dark. "You're going to finish what you've started with me. Right now."

"You don't have the balls to finish!" she shouted at him. Meanwhile fear was taking over her body. She knew that there was no turning back now, and it was too late to plead with him or try and put him in his place.

Her wrists were hurting, and suddenly, as though he had been planning this, a rope appeared, and he began to tie her wrists behind her back. She was down on the grass, on her knees in front of him before she could think to struggle. He held her by the hair, and with his other hand, he pulled out his cock which was hard and throbbing. He ruthlessly forced it in her mouth, down her throat as far as he could thrust it. He let it surge inside her mouth and throat until she was gagging, trying to pull away from him. He would not allow it, pulling her violently against his groin. He rode her hard for an unbearable amount of time, but he did not come, for he had just begun his assault.

When he withdrew his cock, wet with her spit, he pushed her to the ground on her hands and knees.

Liza cringed and churned with desire simultaneously. She felt his strong grip holding her down, and then he brought his palm down hard on her ass and smacked her hard. She screamed at the pain. He brought his hand down again and again, slapping her hard on her creamy, pulsating flesh. Even within his cruelty, his passion was discernable, and despite her pain she was turned on. The wetness of her pussy was apparent as her juices dripped down her legs.

Stephen tore away his clothing, and in a flash he was inside her hot cunt, slamming his cock against her, pumping his hips like a machine. As her cunt opened to receive his tool, her anus tightened, which is precisely what he wanted her body to do. He withdrew from her pussy, still holding her down. His cock was dripping with her juices, and with no more lubrication than her own sweet nectar, he plunged into her asshole. Liza shrieked with the stunning jolt. She'd been taken more times in the ass than she could count, but never by Stephen. She had never allowed him to take her in the ass, and now he was doing it without consent. He was slamming into her so hard and fast that she could not even begin to match his pleasure. He squeezed her tender ass hard and mean, and plowed into it over and over again as Liza's guests watched, mesmerized.

She could feel their eyes on her. She was the center of attention, and someplace deep within her being, a place beyond the pain, there was a hint of joy mingled with her cries of shame.

In one great surge, Stephen began to build to his climax. He pulled Liza's head up by clutching handfuls of hair, and she gasped. There before her sat Oliver, reclining in a lounge, watching with his customary detachment. Yet even in his distant stare, Liza was certain that she could see that he was taking

The Applicant

some pleasure in her defilement. His expression was a reminder to her that he was the one ultimately in control.

Liza closed her eyes. Suddenly she felt humiliated and embarrassed, and as she experienced her shame, the pain in her anus became more acute. She could sense that Stephen was ready to climax, and she silently begged for him to finish quickly. When he was about to come, he did not thrust forward as Liza had expected, but, surprisingly he withdrew his enflamed member and spewed his thick white spunk all over her splayed ass.

There was silence as her body fell to the ground. The cool grass comforted her tender flesh. She felt Stephen rise from behind her. He did not touch her, but simply stood and walked away. Liza looked up in time to catch a subtle exchange of glances pass between Oliver and Stephen.

Oliver rose to his feet at last and approached his wife. He bent down and untied her.

"Liza, get up and go to your room. I think our guests have had enough for this afternoon."

Liza lay back in the tub, attempting to relax. It was difficult because she was completely aroused, and she could not resist playing with her pussy and breasts as she lay there. However, she was too angry to take the pleasure she desired, and her orgasm eluded her, for now.

Outside, the dinner was commencing without her. Oliver was playing the attentive host, and Liza could hear him laughing with his deep-throated voice. Her head fell back against the tub, and she closed her eyes and tried to forget about her recent assault. It made her angry to be reminded by Oliver that he was, in fact, the one in control of the weekend's festivities.

"Liza, your guests are waiting for you." His voice cut through her thoughts.

"Oliver," she replied in surprise. She sat up to look at him and felt her eyes fill with tears. She waited for him to pick her up from the water and make love to her. She wanted nothing more than have him run his hands over her body, to soothe her, touch her, fuck her. She wanted him to stay with her.

"I've not come to comfort you," Oliver stated emotionlessly.

"I need you," she pleaded.

"You got what you wanted, didn't you?"

"Oliver, please ... How am I going to face those people after this afternoon?"

"That's just your wounded pride speaking. Besides, it was a hell of a good show."

"Thanks," she said flatly.

Oliver looked at her and smiled. "I think you'd better repair yourself quickly and get on with the weekend. After all, you have to prepare that sweet young thing for me tomorrow." His voice was a firm, gentle reminder of her duties.

Liza reluctantly stood in the bath and stepped out. She knew it was time to move the weekend to its next scene.

CHAPTER XI

Eleven

Hilary stood at the door of the white house. Her cunt was on fire and had been that way ever since she had received the phone call.

She had left work early and gone home to put on her sluttish costume. She carefully fixed the dildo in her ass and reveled in the deep sensation of pain that came before her inner channel relaxed around the object. She watched herself in the mirror, accomplishing every move slowly so that she could feel all the sensations the dildo afforded her body. She wanted to be thoroughly aroused in every region of her body so that when she finally arrived at her destination, she would be ready.

She sensed that this weekend was going to challenge her far more than the other two had. When she picked up the collar, she lovingly stroked the leather. She brought it to her nostrils and smelled the sweetness and the musky earth and animal smell of it. Her body was moved with earthy passion. She lost herself in a daydream, in which heavy hands probed, invaded, slapped, and kneaded her flesh until she was raw with desire. As she fastened the collar around her supple neck, she understood her utter captivity to her own desires. The collar was a perfect symbol of her submission, and as her loins burned, she wondered what daring acts her mistress and master would force her to do.

The sun was low in the sky, and the porch of the white house was covered in shadows. The vine that crawled around the pillars seemed to suggest hands and arms winding their way about flesh. Hilary inhaled deeply, appreciating the smell of the cool, freshly cut grass. Her body churned on the dildo hidden in her bottom, the cruel hardness of the object violating her last remaining virgin orifice. She knew without a doubt that her asshole would not for long remain untouched by more human instruments.

The door opened at last, and she was let in by the maid, Laura. She followed as the buxom woman led her through the house. Even the decorous maid appeared sensual to Hilary's heightened sensibility. She watched Laura's ass appreciatively as it swayed seductively up the stairs. Laura did not stop at the room on the second floor that Hilary had occupied twice before. Instead, she led her through a short door, which they both had to stoop to make their way through. Beyond the door was a narrow and steep stairway to the attic. It seemed a perfect tenor for the weekend, as Hilary felt a certain Gothic thrill coarse through her body. It was stiflingly hot, and the dank air greeted her as they rose higher and higher within

The Applicant

the mysterious structure. More than once she nearly slipped on the narrow stairs and had to grab the wall for support.

At the top of the staircase was an attic out of childhood fantasies. The dusty room was filled with trunks and wardrobes and old boxes stacked against the walls. There were dressers of a time gone by, an old sewing machine and dress form with yellow chiffon still clinging to it, like a woman still clinging to her youth. Hilary smelled the ancient dust and the hint of mold as well as the polish that made the wooden wardrobes shine. Each step she took into the attic, she shed another portion of her former life. Liza and Oliver had offered her another world that was far more compelling, and Hilary was willing to lose herself in their fantasies and games of pleasure.

As Laura led her toward the front of the house, Hilary saw a door hidden in the wall. The maid pulled a key from her apron and opened the door of the room where Hilary was to stay. There was a single iron bed that had been painted white with a patchwork quilt on top. There was a small wardrobe, and a straight-backed chair sat next to a full-length freestanding mirror. The small window over the bed let in a very little air, so that the room was quite hot and stifling.

"Remove your clothes," Laura instructed her.

The request startled Hilary. It was an unexpected command coming from the maid/cook who had never participated in any of the recent activities. For the first time, Hilary looked at her, not as a servant, but as a woman. There was no hint of seduction on Laura's face, and this clinical expression made it difficult for Hilary to remove her clothes in front of her.

She took off the belt first, and then she carefully pulled the top over her breasts and head. Suddenly

Hilary felt as though she wanted Laura to desire her. Slowly she pulled away the spandex pants and was left standing in front of the expressionless maid with nothing on but the dildo and collar.

"Remove those too," Laura instructed her.

Hilary carefully undid the ribbons that strapped the dildo in place, and it came shooting out of her body. She dropped it into the bag that Laura held out for her. Hilary felt distressed that this woman was taking no interest in her exposure. She wanted Laura to fuck her. She wanted Laura to notice her.

Hilary then dutifully removed the collar, and was disappointed when Laura, having collected her belongings, exited the room without a word or parting glance.

It was too hot to be anything but nude, and Hilary felt her nakedness to be a blessing. The heat of her pussy was intense, and her fingers found the glistening mound of flesh. She began to touch herself with relish. She had kept herself cleanly shaved since the first time Liza had ordered her to remove her pussy hair. She was more naked without pubic hair and she liked the way she felt more exposed and vulnerable. She also liked the way her pussy seemed to exhibit its heat more obviously without hair.

With the dildo gone, there was a hollow feeling in her ass, an emptiness that Hilary yearned to have filled. She bent over in front of the mirror and looked at the little puckered hole. The mirror was a perfect instrument to examine her entire body. She wondered how her asshole would stretch to accommodate the largeness of a man's thrusting cock. She toyed with her asshole and fingered her cunt until she was beginning to move like a bitch in heat before the large glass. She thrust herself on her own arm and finger-fucked herself, shoving three fingers into her

The Applicant

burning twat, as her clit rubbed against her palm and her pussy-lips rubbed against her wrist. She was so hot, so taken by the scene of her hot self-loving session, that she was begging herself for more, until at last when the hard pleasure of sensation was nearly bursting in her body, she stopped herself short, using all her straining will power as she honored her promise to Liza, just at the verge of an intensely explosive, throbbing orgasm.

Yet she knew this near-orgasm was only the very beginning. For what she sought, and to be win her mistress, she knew she needed to wait for the other bodies that would soon be around her. She needed hands and mouths, cocks and pussies to stimulate her, fill her, and bring her off deep, hard and long. She posed before the mirror, her lips parted in a seductive pant, drops of sweat beading on her body. She saw herself as an animal in heat.

She began to consider the room that she was to stay in. She felt quite alone in her little room, with the small bed, the stifling heat and the dank, musty attic air. But most of all, Hilary felt alone with her suspense.

Her body continued to pulse with sexual fever. Every fiber of her being wanted more. She needed more than her own touch could give her. At last, she lay down on the little bed and fell asleep.

"She's here, ma'am."

"Is she in her room?"

"Yes, ma'am."

"Does she appear to be ready?"

"Quite."

"Do you have her things? The collar and dildo and clothes?"

"Yes."

"Do you understand what you are supposed to do, Laura?"

"Yes, ma'am."

"I will let you know when we require her in the morning."

"Good."

Liza dismissed the maid with a smile. She had a fondness for the woman. Whatever pleasure Laura took from the proceedings at the house were her own secret. She suspected that Laura had private passions that kept her busy in her room after hours, but that was her own business and she kept it to herself. For her position at the estate, Liza trusted Laura implicitly. She had a manner of detachment and discretion which aided her in carrying out her tasks with methodical precision.

The guests had sailed the lake after dinner. It was a lazy evening, with light and shadow and wind playing nicely on their bodies. The guests looked forward to returning to the house for the sensual games that they had come to expect from a weekend at the estate.

Liza waited in the house, making last-minute touches on certain details of the ambiance that she wanted her guests to experience. Her anticipation was laced with a vague but nagging feeling of humiliation. This evening would be the first time she had appeared since the episode with Stephen. She knew that she could rise above it, for it was still her game; nothing could change that. She left the bedroom, holding her body erect, sexuality oozing from her regal persona.

"It's a midsummer's night," she said gleefully to her guests as they entered the house after their sojourn on the lake. "So we'll spend the evening in the dark of night on the grounds of the estate. It will be a game of hide and seek. Whomever you find,

The Applicant

whatever you touch is yours. No one shall be permitted to enter the house until morning. We shall sleep as the sun comes up."

Liza's guests looked at her with awed delight. It was no wonder that Oliver had selected her as his mate. Liza spoke her words with force and sensuality, and in doing so, she reestablished her poised position in their minds.

As her guests left the house, they were clothed only in the simplest of coverings. The women wore thongs and gauze frocks, and the men wore only thongs. Of course everyone was aware of the fact that all their clothing would be gone by morning.

This game was one of Liza's favorites. It was a decadent game of tag, and she loved to watch the naked bodies romp. This type of play reminded her of Camelot, and she fancied herself the Guinevere of sexuality when she presided over such raw fun. She loved watching her guests run in and out of the garden and the groves that surrounded the estate. The women allowed themselves to be captured and enjoyed recounting how many hot cocks their willing bodies had accepted before the morning light ended the game. Men enjoyed men, and women, women, for it was a free-for-all and nothing was taboo.

It had not been Liza's thought to join the game that night, and of course Oliver would not because he never did. But she was certain that Oliver was not about to have her in his bed that evening, and she decided at last that she needed the distance that the game of fantasy afforded so that she could forget her troubles and wars of the day.

So at last, she too shed her clothing as soon as her guests had dispersed into the evening shadows. Naked, she sped toward the grove of tall pine trees. The grass beneath her feet made her feel like a sprite, wild and free in the damp evening dew. The forest floor was soft with earth and leaves that served as a cushion for her bare feet. She darted from tree to tree, trying to see by moon and starlight the forms of her guests. Anxious to find her first lover of the evening, she realized that she was ready to devour any flesh that found its way in her path. With all the punishments from Oliver, the passions with Stephen, and the anticipation of Hilary, Liza was the hottest cunt in the forest. She was wet, willing, and waiting to pounce upon her prey!

In the dark room, Hilary lay awake.

There was no light in the little attic room, save the light of the moon, which was adequate. Late in the night, a tray had arrived with simple food and a bottle of red wine to quench the hunger that was growing in her body.

"Laura, do you know when I will be summoned?" she asked.

"No, I do not," said the maid simply, taking the tray from the room. As she closed the door behind her, Hilary noted that she locked it. She was once again plunged into the loneliness of her wait.

She lay back against the pillow on her bed and drifted off to sleep, feeling slightly drunk from the wine. She could've sworn she heard the distant sounds of laugher, but she knew that she had to be dreaming.

She closed her eyes and drifted into a state where her unconscious could reel pictures in her mind. In her visions she saw an ancient courtly setting, where ladies and lords frolicked in the moonlight; a castle was in the background. She could hear the ladies giggle and the men laugh as they chased one another. She realized they were naked, and that there were bodies of all shapes and sizes.

The Applicant

The restrictive garments of the time—the ironlike corsets and the codpieces—were strewn across a beautiful green field and upon rocks at a nearby stream. The bodies ran and played in the field, chasing one another behind bushes. And the stream was alive with naked men and women. They were all playing in provocative ways.

One man was on his hands and knees, covered with water from the waist down, sensually tonguing the belly button of a beautifully plump and juicy woman who soon opened her large legs and let his tongue into her twat. Hilary could see the woman's fat pussy-lips gleam, could see the tongue travel the length of the cunt lips and then dart into a wet, waiting, extremely juicy hole.

Another couple was in the reverse position. The man was holding the head of a maiden who was sucking his cock, and the woman's body swayed to the sensual feel of the stream trickling by her as she devoured the large shaft that pumped in and out of her mouth.

Not far from those four, a woman was hanging from a tree branch that protruded into the stream, and two men held her legs wide apart as a second woman dove her tongue deliciously into the very exposed pussy. Hilary could see the tongue move gingerly around the thin cunt lips. She watched as the woman who performed this cunnilingus began to take the top of the woman's pussy into her mouth, gently suckling on the golden pubic hairs and the upper pussy flesh and clit. She inserted a finger and the woman groaned and seemed to hang precariously from the tree limb, her arms becoming weak from the pleasure of her cunt. Hilary thought she would drop, but then she could see the woman's hands were bound, and part of her deep pleasure was the pain of the ropes that held her wrists to the tree. The woman exuded loud, uninhibited, animal-like noises as her pussy received delicious, extravagant licks, all the while being held apart by the two men, who were clearly hard and hot from doing their job; their cocks stood out, just above the height of the water.

Hilary's cunt was responding to her dream, and she began gyrating without consciously realizing it; her body seemed to experience the pleasure of her sleeping fantasy. This nearly roused her, but then she was called back into the dream.

Her vision traveled down the stream to a place where an elegant woman was just about to open her legs to a man who wore a ram's head mask over his head and eyes. Hilary noticed that the horns of the mask were shaped very much like a man's cock. Her dream then rewound to the moments prior. She saw that the masked man had chased the woman for many yards. The woman had run faster than the wind, giggling, but finally he caught her and tossed her on the soft grass. He brought himself down on her, kissing her neck, her tits, her lips, penetrating her mouth with his tongue. Then he bent between her smooth, creamy thighs and took what was now his, devouring her completely. The tongue plunged into the sweet hole as if dipping into a honey pot; it licked the long cunt shaft and nibbled the sweet clitoris. He kissed at her pussy mound and then returned his tongue to her clitoris, sucking the tiny bud until the woman writhed in obvious pleasure and desire.

Then he stopped, hoisted himself between her legs, and readied a huge, unbelievably fat cock at the opening of the woman's cunt. Hilary got a close-up of the regal-looking woman and realized it was Liza who was getting fucked by a man with a ram's mask.

The Applicant

He parted the thighs wide, and with his hand, brought the huge weapon to her wet opening. He plunged in and Liza flinched; he was so big, he nearly ripped her. Liza immersed herself in the pain and pleasure. She thrust her hips up to greet him, moving in unison with his big, hard, thrusting cock. She brought the man to a wild, wicked climax; he screamed like an animal as his come shot from the huge head of his prick. He pulled out and shot it on her smooth belly, then slid the still-hard cock all over her flesh, rubbing the joy juice into her skin.

Next, his head was between her legs again, and this time he was fucking her with the ram's head, inserting the cock-shaped animal horn into her twat. Her groin lifted and pressed into the horn, and in the dream, Hilary could see the horn move in and out, wet with Liza's cunt juice. Suddenly, two young women appeared and sprinkled flowers around Liza, as her body twitched with untold passion, her cunt getting fucked by the animal horn, the motions just like a battering ram. The man made noise as he fucked, and the maidens bent down on either side of Liza and began to massage her titties and suck the nipples. Liza grew heavy with lust, and her body twitched with longing. The man took a finger to her clit and rubbed hard, as he battered her pussy with the horn. Suddenly, a noise rose from Liza's belly and through her throat. She screamed a scream of passion and pain as the man with the ram's horn fucked and fucked and fucked away at her pussy, rubbing her clit until the explosion could not be delayed.

Liza came like a wild woman, the orgasm shooting out of her cunt and up her asshole and spine. Hilary could feel it rushing through her own groin. As the man of the dream kissed Liza's spent pussy and licked up her golden dew, Hilary's own finger was in her own pussy. Even though she was forbidden to come when her mistress was not there to watch, Hilary's unconscious mind and desires could not be contained. Her red hot cunt exploded with her dream. Finally, she slept.

"You're caught!" the voice whispered in her ear. Suddenly there were a pair of powerful arms around Liza, embracing her in a swift movement that had her on her back in seconds.

She reveled in the feel of this man on top of her, and her legs wrapped around the small of his back immediately. As he lowered his stiffened cock into her cunt, she could sense the powerful thighs beginning to propel them towards a wild fuck. She loved the feel of his balls slapping her anus, increasing her pleasure greatly. She lifted her breasts so that his hands could play with her nipples. He put his mouth to them, and took her breasts in his strong hands, squeezing her with bites and pinches that sent her loins surging. He rode her hard, and she lifted her hips to meet him thrust for thrust, pressing her pelvis to his so that she could take him deeper and deeper still inside her flaming pussy. She grabbed his cock with her cunt and pulled it inside her.

"Fuck me harder," she begged him, biting his neck fiercely as she felt her orgasm growing deep within her abdomen. "Oh harder, fuck harder, please!" She gasped for air as her cry of orgasmic pleasure cut through the heavy air of the wood. His pleasure was a scream from deep within his gut; a loud bestial sound. Together they let the tensions of their bodies spill into the world of night that surrounded them.

As she lay there for a moment, with his heaving body over her, Liza could hear the sounds of voices echoing in the dark. It was soothing music to her

The Applicant

ears, and it sumptuously satisfied her. He pulled himself out of her as he lightly caressed her sweating flesh. Over and over again, his hands manipulated her body, touching every part of her so that her body rose and fell in one spasm after another, her passion mounting and declining into the earth where she lay, her legs wide open to receive his touch.

And then rather suddenly, he stood and ran into the darkness of the trees.

The leaves around her comforted her for a moment of quiet. Soon enough she would stand and run off to find herself another body to please and to give her pleasure. But for the time being she lay staring up into the dark. She sighed, relieved that the delicate equilibrium of her weekend was restoring itself.

CHAPTER XII

Twelve

While her room was still dark, Hilary heard the sound of birds, the soft music of morning as the sun beckoned her to rise from her bed and look out the little attic window. It was still not completely light out, but the sun was shining on the tops of the trees, and the grass on the far side of the lawn was starting to gleam with the morning dew. She felt the slight breeze of cool air and it teased her warm flesh. The wind seemed to stir the flame of her already raging desire, a desire that had been fueled by dangerous dreams. All night long, as she lay half-waking, the sound of voices drifted in through the small window. Hilary could only guess at what the sounds meant; she could only imagine what brought on the sexual screams throughout the evening.

Strawberries, juice, and tea cakes arrived after the sun had come out completely and the day was well on its way to starting. Laura was again completely silent, making her quick delivery of food and then leaving again locking the door behind her.

Hilary watched herself in the mirror as she ate, for her reflection was her only companion in the room. She studied herself, admiring the curves and sensuous lines of her body. She gazed for a long time at her soft cunt, marveling at the gentle folds of flesh and the way it puckered invitingly. The heat inside her rose in full measure, and she felt sure that she could have multiple orgasms if she simply reached between her legs and gave her self a good fingering. But she wanted to wait; she wanted to savour the anticipation. The dream of the night before was now buried in her subconscious mind.

As morning dawned on the rest of the estate, the guests of Liza's wild sexual games made their way to the house where they found beds waiting for them. They all fell quickly to sleep, having spent enormous amounts of energy the night before in an orgy that lasted for as many hours as there was darkness.

Liza's night had ended much earlier than that of the rest of her guests; after her fourth fucking encounter she found her way to bed and collapsed next to Oliver.

Her guests would sleep long and rise later in the day. Upon waking, Liza considered Hilary for a moment, wondering if she was miserable alone and waiting in her attic room with a wide-open, hot, pink pussy. Liza remembered all too well how miserable that could be, forced to wait, with your cunt on fire with sex heat so intense your own hand—no matter how skilled—could never quench the flames. But

The Applicant

then Liza smiled, knowing how well Hilary would be primed for the pleasures that awaited her.

She heard the key in the lock at last. It had to be Liza, Hilary thought; she could wait no longer for her mistress. Her heart began to race, as she could hardly wait to gaze into Liza's green eyes. She had seen her in her dreams all night long. In her dreams she had kissed her mistress' lips ravenously, caressing the woman's tits and licking her cunt all night long. All the while Oliver's dark, mysterious eyes watched them make love.

Unfortunately, it was Laura who entered the room; Hilary's vision was shattered.

"You are to be readied now, miss," she said.

The woman handed her soap and a washcloth and towel. She poured water from the pitcher into the large basin that stood on a little vanity table, which suggested to Hilary that she was to sponge herself clean in Laura's presence. Once again she felt the urge to seduce this unmovable woman. She proceeded to gently touch the cloth to her body, and because the water was cold, her nipples became instantly erect. She felt her clit flutter as she passed the wash cloth between her legs. She never took her eyes off Laura's, and Laura returned the stare. But her eyes were emotionless.

As Hilary dried herself with the towel, Laura left the room for a moment and returned with a small cart. On the top shelf was an enema bag.

"This is not pleasant, miss," was all Laura said.

The woman was a master of precision and orderliness. She displayed no warmth, no trace of anything but her concentration on the thoroughness of her task. Hilary watched as Laura filled the the bag.

"Lie down," commanded the maid.

Hilary lay down on the bed while Laura inserted the large plastic nozzle in her tiny asshole. The maid had already prepared her rear for the penetration, so it was hardly a shock. Hilary could feel the fluid flowing into her cavity, and the sense of being filled gave her a great sense of pleasure despite the discomfort. She recognized this as simply another way of increasing her anticipation for what was to come.

"You are to hold this for five minutes," Laura said.

Hilary endured each minute in compelling discomfort, trying desperately not to spill any liquid too soon, while the maid sat in the chair and ticked off the minutes on her watch. When the time was up, Laura placed the chamber pot in the middle of the room, removing the rug to a corner where it would not be soiled in the event of a mishap.

"You may relieve yourself," Laura instructed.

To her surprise, Hilary made her way to the receptacle without accident, and deposited the water and all it had gathered. She felt immensely relieved, and letting go of all the liquid gave her a great sense of pleasure and release. She had never had an enema before, but something told her that this would not be the last one she would receive.

After cleaning herself, Hilary stood in the center of the room, wondering what was to come next. Laura retrieved a small amber bottle from a tray on the cart and began to rub Hilary's body with a sweet-smelling oil. The maid smeared the oil on her, sliding fingers in between her ass cheeks, and then between her thighs and on up to her belly and her breasts. Hilary's body was aroused, and she felt frustrated that the other woman was interested in only completing her task.

When she had finished, Laura fastened Hilary into a very tight bustier that was black and stiff with bon-

The Applicant

ing. It held her tightly about the ribs beneath her breasts so that her waist seemed tiny and her breasts and hips much larger. Her tits were pushed up and out so that, as Hilary peered into the mirror, she looked twice her normal size. Laura then held out a tiny thong panty that was also black, and once Hilary slipped it on, she turned to see that it was simply a black triangle of fabric that barely covered her pussy and left her ass completely exposed. Next Laura held out a new collar. It was similar to the one Hilary had worn before, but this one was made of the softest kid leather and it conformed easily to her neck. It was much thicker in width however, and as Laura fixed it around her, Hilary felt a thrill of submissive pleasure electrify her body.

All these ministrations seemed designed to build and fan Hilary's inner fires, and the collar made her feel as though she were going to explode with passion. Around the collar's width were rings that could be used in thousands of ways to ensure her servitude and bondage; the rings clanked together and against the leather, creating a sound that sent a rapid jolt of anxiety and fear through her body.

Lastly, Laura placed six-inch black stiletto heels in front of her. Hilary stepped into them, completing her outfit of submission. She looked in the mirror and admired how her ass was exposed, how her feet were captured by the shoes, and how her crotch was framed within the black silk of the thong. She admired the way her tits thrust forward, beckoning the attentions of anyone who saw them.

"One more thing, miss." Laura reached into the bag and withdrew the paddle that Hilary had come to know so well. "The master wants your ass well reddened." Laura pulled the chair away from the corner as she said, "Bend over it, miss."

Hilary obeyed and bent over the wooden seat.

"Farther forward please."

Hilary squirmed forward so that her breasts were centered on the seat.

"Hold still."

The first smacks of the leather paddle were firm, but not unbearable. The blows covered all the softest fleshy parts of her rump. Once her ass had been thoroughly covered not once, but twice, with Laura's strong strokes, Hilary felt the alarming sting of an enflaming liquid that the maid applied to her bottom. Then Laura began to paddle her again, this time in earnest. She did not spare her strength, but pulled her arm back far and raised the paddle high and with full force, forcefully whacking at Hilary's bottom.

"Oh, god," pleaded Hilary, "please stop. It hurts too much ... please ... please ..."

Laura ignored her plea.

The paddle came down hard, in rapid succession. Laura peppered Hilary's bottom with enough whacks to make the pain nearly unbearable. Just when Hilary thought that she might start to scream, the maid ceased firing. Tingling pain traversed Hilary's body, as Laura rested her arms and sighed at her job well done.

And then, as soon as the torment was over, Hilary was covered once again with the liquid that burnt and enflamed her already-stinging flesh.

"That will make the redness stay," explained Laura, whose face was as red as Hilary's bottom from the hard work.

Hilary was nearly dizzy, and it took her a minute to regain her composure and breath. When she stood, she reeled and almost fell, the spike heels making it difficult to walk. Yet as she rose, she could feel the unmistakable twinge of turn-on between her

The Applicant

legs; dipping one finger along the inner lips of her pussy, she could feel the wetness covering the swelling sex flesh.

"Look at your bottom," Laura commanded.

Hilary turned and gasped as she saw her ass wild and pink with swelling and marks.

"That's a proper ass to present to master Oliver."

Hilary felt a kind of silent glory that she had succeeded in coming this far in her journey as a submissive. She felt honored.

The snap of a leash fastening to her collar broke her reverie, and Laura jerked her chain, leading her from the room. Hilary realized that the drama was, at last, beginning.

CHAPTER XIII

Thirteen

The guests were all gracious, and grateful, about the big fuck game played the night before. Of course, when they gathered that following day, it was an orgy of recognition, with everyone trying to figure out who fucked whom in the darkness the night before. They were smiling at one another knowingly, talking, touching, and acknowledging the great fun had by all.

One of Liza's fucks was a beautiful blonde named Stella, whose very hot and juicy cunt made a delicious receptacle for Liza's fist the night before. Stella had howled like a dog as her cunt was filled by Liza's fingers; she reciprocated by eating out the mistress of the house, in the front and the back, so that both Liza's holes were filled with lips, tongue, and fingers.

Perhaps the most deliciously striking moment in

their encounter was a French kiss that lasted far longer than most fucks. The two women, standing breast to breast, nipple to nipple, kissed for a long, luxurious time and felt each other's bodies up and down before getting down to fucking and sucking. In a way, Liza was fucking Stella lovingly, as if compensating for her unfulfilled desires to have her sweet slave Hilary.

Stella approached Liza with a smile the next day.

"It was a fabulous night," Stella said to Liza, as she pulled her aside and gave her a long kiss on the lips, flicking her tongue in Liza's mouth seductively, recalling their kiss of the night before

"There's more where that came from, darling," Liza replied, returning the kiss with relish.

Adam came up from behind and put his hand on Liza's ass while she continued to kiss Stella.

"I had you last night behind the stable. You were magnificent," he whispered in her ear.

Liza stopped kissing Stella and said, "Was that you?" She remembered well being rammed with his big cock and feeling satisfied when it was over.

All three of them laughed.

There was a laziness that filled the warm room as the guests lounged, recounting their adventures and fantasies to one another. The women wore elegant silks and the fabric, like their banter, floated about them in the smoky air. There were whispered seductions, and speculations about what was to follow in the next scene of the drama. There was a subdued energy in the room. It was as though everyone present was saving their energy for the future, and this added to the quality of repressed anxiety and pleasure in the room. Suddenly the door opened and there she stood.

All eyes were drawn to the woman who had entered the room.

The Applicant

Liza stood in the corner, waiting as anxiously as her guests for Hilary's arrival. She remembered how it had felt to stand on the other side of that door. When at last the door opened, Liza turned to see the rare creature that she had created—the woman that might be capable of charming her husband's friends, just as *she* had two years ago.

She saw Hilary standing there, a woman provocative because of the fact that she was bound and tethered by her body's desires. Liza saw triumph standing before her, for she knew then that Hilary would not let her down. She had succeeded in creating a lover suitable for herself and her husband.

Hilary looked at the guests in the room with some fear, but she continued to carry herself regally, with her head held high and her breasts pushed forward. She was ready to offer herself and her freedom.

Hilary's eyes met Liza's, and her passions leapt to her throat, the fire consuming her body. She met Liza's stare with a stance of strength and knowing that she would serve her mistress well—she would serve her very well indeed. And she would serve her master just as well.

In the stable he dismounted from the pale gray stallion.

"Easy friend," Oliver said to the magnificent animal as it pawed the ground. "I shall return tonight." He stroked the horse's rump and flanks for a moment, and nuzzled the soft white nose. He felt bonded to the powerful animal, for they were of the same wild breed.

Oliver stepped out of the stable and walked toward the house. He continued to carry the riding crop that he was accustomed to taking on his rides.

The whip dangled by his boots as he walked up the stoney path that led to the house.

"Let us see your ass," Liza commanded.

Hilary turned.

"Bend forward."

She did as she was ordered, placing her hands on her knees so that her ass was clearly in view to everyone in the room. The flesh of her buttocks was still fiery, and there were pink stripes still raised on her tender skin.

"Get up."

Hilary rose and faced her mistress. Their eyes met, and it seemed there was an intense moment of silent communion between them. Then Liza's eyes turned hard and her expression stern.

Hilary was certain that it was at last the hour in which she would meet Oliver face to face. She could sense his presence near. Her mind crowded with thoughts of being fucked by him in front of all these strangers, and the vision made her cunt waken and flutter.

"Hilary," Liza said. "You have one hour to satisfy each guest in this house. Do not fail in your task." The command given, Liza turned and left the room.

Hilary was stunned, for this was not at all what she had imagined. She looked around at the strange faces. No one moved, and she realized that they were going to be animated by her presence. This thought bolstered her courage, and she looked about the room. Her sight landed on an elegant woman reclining gracefully on a lounge. Her eyes, unlike the other women present, were not hard or malicious. This woman's eyes were soft and seductive. Hilary decided to begin with her.

She got down on her hands and knees and crawled

The Applicant

toward Stella, as a good submissive should. She pushed her ass high in the air and jutted her chest out so that all present could admire her body. She moved with eyes down toward Stella, whose flowing black silk robe lay partly open, revealing a firm breast.

As she reached Stella, Hilary looked at her beautiful body clothed under the clinging fabric. She admired that outline of the woman's sumptuous thighs and her blonde pussy. Hilary carefully moved the robe aside and lay her hands on Stella's warm flesh. As she put her mouth to one of Stella's nipples and sucked, she fingered the blonde pussy, which was already wet and hot. Stella's head dropped back against the cushion as Hilary nibbled and sucked one nipple, then the other, continuing all the while to gently tease the plump folds of her swollen cunt and clit. Hilary moved her mouth down Stella's body, kissing her belly and her thighs. At last she knelt before the woman and put her tongue to Stella's sex. She began to eat her out with a hunger she had never known before. She sucked her clitoris and teased the ripe lips of Stella's cunt. She shoved her tongue inside her and fucked her with her mouth. Hilary's ass began to mimic the wild gyrations of Stella's hips, and she pushed her tongue in deeper and deeper into the woman's cunt, and then withdrawing, she suckled and licked her clit. Hilary ferociously poured her energy into the other woman's body, so that it was only minutes before Stella was screaming with pleasure, bucking violently under her kisses.

Hilary moved with a new kind of grace, her mouth moving from drinking the sweet juices of Stella's cunt, to taking cocks that offered themselves to her as she crawled on hands and knees. With a hunger that would not be sated until she had tasted and fucked every cock and pussy in the room, she found the first stiff cock that was in her path. Her tongue and lips teased the head as it grew full. She circled the shaft, relishing the taste. Then she took the prick in her mouth, swallowing it all the way to the balls and there she let the male rhythm take over, roughly fucking her mouth. Like Stella, the man attached to the cock was already aroused and came in a few minutes. Hilary gladly drank every last drop of his spunk as it poured down her open throat.

In automatic abandon, she moved to the next. She had no conception of time, place, or the identity of whoever she was fucking, sucking, eating, or licking. She went from one to another, sucking pussy, sucking cock, sucking tits. She tasted whatever was offered and took into her cunt or her mouth whoever wished to take her. She knew she must have had some guests several times over, and certainly she'd had them all. It was hard for her to know, for she had become delirious in the desire to serve her mistress well by serving her mistress's guests *very* well.

She was on her knees before a handsome cock, her tongue lapping the head with rapid fire. Hilary felt at times that she could continue on forever, never stopping, taking cock after cock, pussy after pussy until she dropped with exhaustion. As her own body screamed with need, and as she remained unsatisfied, she felt that she was in a constant state of preorgasmic tension. She was enjoying the height of sensitivity and energy that was making her body feel as though it were truly an entity unto itself, while her consciousness lingered elsewhere. She felt that at any instant she would be ready to spill over the edge into pleasing herself, but she waited. She was waiting for her master and mistress.

The cock was pulsing in and out of her mouth, and she was melting into the heat of his rhythm. Like the

The Applicant

others, she was prepared to take his come in her mouth and swallow it greedily. The man groaned with passion and shot his load straight down her throat, and Hilary lapped up the excess that spewed out of the top of his enflamed member, wanting nothing but more, more, more.

"Your ass is pale." She heard his voice and she stopped instantly, keeping her eyes on the floor. She could see his black riding boots and nothing more.

"Turn it to me," he ordered. His voice was like distant thunder, threatening to explode, but controlled at the same time.

Without rising, Hilary turned herself to place her ass at her master's service.

"Higher, bitch," he demanded.

Naturally, she complied.

And then suddenly, Hilary felt his riding crop. It hit her flesh hard, with a pain more searing in its intensity than any she had ever known. And that blow was followed by more strokes. She had never experienced anything quite so intense. When he had finished, Hilary's heart was beating furiously and her breath was short. She was expecting more, but there was a respite, so she kept her head down and waited. She felt him circle her body, and he flicked her lightly with the whip one more time. She jerked in reflex, but she had not betrayed her mistress by crying out once. It had been a tremendously difficult task not to scream as the whip met her flesh, but she had held her peace. A tiny gasp escaped her mouth, and he heard it; this set him to planting another fierce stroke on her enflamed skin. He would not tolerate her crying out in any form, no matter how mild.

When he was finished, he strode around her kneeling figure one more time.

"On your knees," he commanded.

She pulled herself slowly to her knees. She was trembling, terrified by his mysterious force and the potency of his sexual energy. Slowly, she raised her eyes to his face. Oliver ... at last.

His eyes cut her gaze like a razor. They seared her, yet she could not tear her gaze from his, and thus stayed at attention. Hilary knelt down in front of her master.

Liza witnessed it all. She stood opposite the two, watching their movements. Their forceful, vibrant energies clashed as they locked into a private combat that no one else could share. It was an auspicious beginning, thought Liza. She saw how deliberately Oliver walked around the girl, how intent his focus was on her body. She could sense that he was growing hard with lust; she saw the flame in his eyes, the muted fires of animal passion that ruthlessly burned in his expression of desire.

Hilary was his. She was captivated—imprisoned by that lust which made her own desire soar as she clearly recognized her master, her dominant.

As Liza stood unnoticed in the corner, she was suddenly filled with a jealous panic. Not being the object and center of attention was an unfamiliar place for her. Giving Hilary to Oliver was the most profound submissive action she had ever followed through with. To offer Oliver the woman whom Liza desired above all others, to give Hilary to Oliver to use as he pleased, was the most terrifying thing she'd ever undertaken. And then to be forced to stand in the shadows and watch their animal desire pour onto one another was indeed submissive. The worst feeling was the wave of nostalgia that came over Liza. It seemed more than two years ago that she had been kneeling at Oliver's feet, her body and face ragged

The Applicant

from servicing his friends. She remembered the way Oliver had drawn her in, how he had devoured her. Liza knew that she had created a bond with Oliver when she gazed at him in that wild, savage state. It was the essence of their union, their marriage, and it was a flame they renewed again and again.

Liza trembled with the fear that her position as his wife, lover, and slave was about to be usurped. Liza looked at Hilary's body, with its youthful curves and lines. She looked at the beautiful definition of Hilary's breasts and buttocks, and Liza realized that the younger woman had an animal hiding within her that was more fearsome than her own. Hilary had a quality of rawness, something that was not a part of Liza's character. There was an essential difference between the two of them, and it was that difference that she feared would captivate Oliver and draw his attentions away from her.

"Her task has not been completed," Liza suddenly announced. Her voice was more harsh than she meant it to be.

"And what is the task?" Oliver asked, turning to face his wife.

"She was to satisfy ..."

"No," he interrupted Liza, "I want her to tell me."

His rudeness jolted Liza.

"I did not know that I had not completed my task. Certainly I satisfied these people." There was a hint of insolence in her words, and Liza hoped, in that moment, that it would not go unnoticed.

"Is there someone in this room that she hasn't taken?" Oliver looked around at the guests who lounged in various states of undress. They appeared to be content and relaxed.

"Only me, I believe," Diana cooed, as she wound her impressive form to the front of the group. She was like a vulture that had held back just to see if Hilary had enough awareness to know whom she had—and whom she hadn't—fucked. "I think this crowd has been far too easy on her. It seems to me she expects to be waited on, and even serviced." She spit out her words with venomous delight, knowing they would not be lost on Oliver.

For once Liza felt in league with Diana. She knew Diana had held purposely to the corner of the room, and she knew why. Diana shared Liza's desire to cast any wrinkle on the perfection of Hilary.

Oliver quickly glanced from Diana, to Liza, and then to Hilary. There was a moment's pause as he chose his words carefully.

"It seems there are two failures in this room. There will be two prices to pay." His eyes were cold as he spoke.

Hilary did not understand what he meant, but she trembled with fear at his proclamation.

"We'll see how well you bear up to your punishment," he said, looking directly at Hilary.

The young woman was awed at the amount of terror she could bear, and even more surprised at how much pleasure the fear gave her. She also felt betrayed by Liza and Diana, and anger welled up within her despite her fear.

Liza was considering Oliver's words, knowing what he meant. They were precisely chosen words, calculated to hit their mark. Liza could never ignore such an an obvious statement, and his words shook her with such force that she, too, quaked with fear. Oliver was always authentic; he never hid his anger. Liza despaired as her control of the weekend slipped from her hands. She waited breathlessly for his next move.

His eyes were fixed on Hilary. There was a kind of

The Applicant

controlled violence about him that frightened everyone in the room, especially Hilary. Suddenly he turned and walked away. The whip still dangled in his hand, and Hilary still knelt in her place. He roughly pushed the sofa, and with his foot he dragged a stool to the center of the room. He reached down, grabbed Hilary, and unceremoniously threw her down against the stool so that her head and tits were thrust harshly against the red leather.

"Hand me a leather," he demanded.

Someone quickly handed him a long length of brown leather strapping. He deftly ran it under the stool, quickly securing Hilary's back so that her awkward position on the stool would remain so until she was released. The stool forced her ass in the air, and there was no doubt in anyone's mind what Oliver was preparing to do. He knelt behind her and pushed her legs wide apart. He greased her ass, taking a large dollop of lubricant from a jar on the table. He smoothed it all over her crack, rubbing softly, then more aggressively, against her tightly puckered asshole. He slowly began to press his thumb against the opening, lightly at first, and then fiercely, until her ass muscles began to twitch and clench, and finally open. He held the thumb in there, and Hilary could feel the fullness of his finger opening, opening, opening her ... Instinctively, she began to press herself against his thumb, her body begging for more.

"Do not move," Oliver's authoritative voice boomed. To punctuate his point, he suddenly shoved his thumb into her all the way and just as quickly pulled it out. Her ass muscles twitched for more, but he simply studied her butt with his eyes, noticing again the pink marks across her rump, then gazing with great interest at her anus. With two thumbs, he spread her ass flesh apart and exposed her opening fully, until her once-puckered orifice was a gaping opening. He inhaled the scent of her, a natural odor mixed with the lubricant he had so efficiently oiled her with. With his two hands, he held apart the flesh and opened her as widely as he could; Hilary felt the flesh begin to pull apart, as if her crack was being torn ever so slightly. The excitement registered in her cunt, but she wasn't prepared when Oliver suddenly jerked her ass cheeks apart even further. And then, without pause, he pulled out his hard cock and plunged it straight into her ass.

She gasped, but she did not cry out. Hilary bore down as she had learned to do, and fell back upon his cock, wanting to take her master as deep as he could ram it into her. Oliver held her tightly at the thighs as he thrust forward. Hilary was certain that she was being split in two.

Liza watched him fuck her, and she wished it was *her* punishment. In watching Hilary, Liza had come back around, and now she found herself pleading for Hilary to hold on so that they could at last be together. Liza silently pleaded with Hilary to stay quiet so that Oliver would deem her worthy—deem them both worthy.

Diana watched Oliver fucking the young wench, despising what she could not have, regardless of the fact that she had been the catalyst of this drama. She realized that she was as much a tool of Oliver's as anyone else, though she often wished to believe otherwise.

Oliver's groans rose above the room, a deafening tribute to the way he pounded into Hilary's ass, his balls slapping up against her cunt. He took his time fucking her, for the sensation of taking her last orifice of virginity was too delicious to rush. His fervor rose and fell in thunderous waves, taking him to the edge,

The Applicant

but not over it. He thrust in and out of her, pressing his fullness into her tight receptacle until he could hold back no longer. Her asshole was opening and closing around his throbbing prick, and it was sucking the come from him. He chose to surrender to the explosion. With one forceful push, he pumped his come into her, holding her butt firmly against his groin so he could totally ram it to her.

His head was back and his eyes closed and the ecstasy flowing through him; it poured down and covered Hilary. His pleasure extended to everyone in the room as he pumped her twice, three, four more times, letting every bit of himself drain into her body. Everyone around responded vicariously, feeling the sex juice that flowed from Oliver's cock to Hilary's asshole. They were swept into the sexual charge that electrified the room

Hilary had given up all pretense of pain; waves of pleasure had mounted in her as they had never done before. She was at a peak of climax so intense that she had never known anything like it before.

But then he was done, and he pulled out of her and pushed her away from him like a piece of used flesh. He wiped his cock with his handkerchief and left the room. The door closed behind him with a definite finality.

Hilary was left with a burning desire, her pussy-lips swollen and her clitoris hard and seeking relief. Her asshole felt strangely empty—but at least she had fulfilled Oliver. At least, she hoped she had.

CHAPTER XIV

Fourteen

He stood in the stable, listening as the Appaloosa stamped and whinnied, crying to be released to run in the meadows of the estate, stamping for his master to come and ride him into the wind of the impending storm as it thundered across the sky.

There was an eerie glow cast above the cumulus of clouds—a combination of the setting sun and the pervading darkness—and a light breeze stirred the dust and leaves with a warm wind that hinted of things to come.

It was as if nature had created an atmosphere just for him, to suit his pleasure and his mood. He smiled, feeling as though he were even controlling *her*—the great Mother Nature.

He was quick to jump up on the broad, bare back

of the horse and ride out of the stable and into the wind. His black hair flowed with a fury, in rhythm with the tail and mane of the beast. It was like a scene from a Gothic novel—man and beast riding off into the storm, a sense of darkness, passion, and drama in the air. Oliver loved the feeling of animal power beneath his loins, and he urged the horse to greater speeds.

He was thinking about the evening.

Liza waited in her room, reeling out of control, while Hilary waited in hers, relinquished.

The guests waited about the house and pool, speculating about what was to come next.

Stephen peered up to Liza's window, and he saw her staring down at him. She had never looked more beautiful. In her present quandary, Stephen knew she was thriving. She was loving the excitement and drama, loving the unexpected twists and turns that the day was taking.

Diana waited. She waited for her own moment of triumph to be witnessed by all.

A wild thunder rattled the windows of the house. Lightning incessantly flashed across the stable room. They had all gathered here for the next scene in this lavish passion play.

Liza arrived at the stable in black leather. By her own choice, she flaunted her body. She was wary with a fear of what lay within the night's offering. Her body was tightly corseted in a garment made of thin strips of soft leather, woven so that her flesh peeked through. It pushed her bodice high and accentuated her beautifully rounded breasts. Her dark nipples stood out like two delicious cherries. The corset came

The Applicant

to a point in front, like an arrow, pointing out her clean, sweet pussy beneath. In the back, the leather stopped just short of her crack. She wore no stockings, only black patent spikes that pushed her ass in the air and made her body more willowy and gracefully regal. Her eyes were made up in the darkest greens and purple, her colored lids extending to her well made up brow. Her cheeks were darkly flushed and her lips painted with a fiery red color. She was wildly crowned with a reddish glow from her hair that made her appear like a wild phantom in the shadows of the dark stable. She knew no matter what the punishment, no matter how he punished her body, she would be queen of the night.

Oliver was tying up his mount when she opened the stable door. He glimpsed her in the shadows moving toward the tack room, looking more cat than woman. His eyes acknowledged her rare beauty.

Inside the tack room, she moved in the wildly flashing light, directly toward Hilary, who sat obediently in the corner. Hilary wore a red leather corset much like Liza's and nothing else but red spiked heels. Laura had been ordered to bring her there at nightfall. When she approached her slave, she yanked hard on the leash that was attached to Hilary's collar. Liza swiftly fastened her to a tether that dangled from the ceiling beside one of the two massive pillars bisecting the room. She pushed Hilary against the cold stone column and grabbed her wrists, fastening them behind her so that her breasts jutted forward.

The girl had proven worthy, though not as mistress of the house. There could only be one mistress, and Liza would not be usurped.

As Liza admired the handsome figure of Hilary tethered and helpless, an insecure feeling came over her. Could Hilary possibly take her place as mistress of the house? She suspected that there were still more surprising events to come before the night was over, and she was feeling wary of the unknown. Liza still felt passion for Hilary, and in her heart awaited the moment when she herself could claim her female prize. But human nature being what it is, Liza succumbed to thoughts of insecurity. "They are just fears," she kept telling herself. "They are not reality."

It took only moments to secure the slave, and when Liza was done, she backed into the opposite pillar and called for Stephen to secure her as well. It was a necessary act to illustrate her own submission. The stone was cold against her ass, and Liza relished the sensation. Her full chest was thrust forward like Hilary's, and Liza's breath heaved in and out with anticipation and wonder. She felt Stephen's rough hands tighten the rope, and she detected a hint of victory in his eyes. But what Stephen would never understand is that Liza really was the master of her own fate, that despite her occasional insecurities, she was a powerful woman who made choices at every turn.

"That won't be necessary, Stephen," he said, his words shattering the ritualized silence in the room. "Untie her."

Stephen did as he was ordered.

Oliver reached out, and in one swift movement, ripped a cat-o'-nine-tails from the wall. Holding it by its leather handle, he held it out to his wife.

"Dance," he ordered.

Liza stared at him, eyes wide with surprise. She smiled inwardly at his masterful stroke of genius. He had a way of using everything and everyone to his advantage, and dancing was something that most befitted Liza's talent and position.

She took the "cat," its talons dancing in the pale

The Applicant

darkness. The lightning and thunder had diminished, and the stable was lit by candles. Using the whip as her partner, she spread it across her thighs and between her legs, dragging it slowly through the crack of her bare pussy. She let its many tails entwine her body like serpents. And then, with a swift change, she brought the whip down across her own buttocks so that the sting made her move with a more heated frenzy. She undulated back and forth, the cat whipping about her frame as she moved. Her arms were like tentacles extending, allowing the leather to jerk back with a swiftness that meant certain pain when it made contact against her flesh. The pain made her more bold, more alluring. She was experienced at turning pain to her advantage, and tonight would be no exception. The harder she brought the whip down upon her flesh, the hotter her pussy became, and the higher her passion soared.

The slaps were like music, and she moved to the syncopated beat of whip touching flesh. It was as if she'd orchestrated it perfectly when a pelting rain outside began to add to the music of her dance. She looked like a vision from a dream—half woman, half cat. It was a primal moment and Liza lost herself in it as she lost control of her body. She began to drown in the pleasures she was giving to herself, her guests, her slave, and her husband. She was getting closer to coming—her finale—and no one dared look away. Her head fell back anticipating the pleasure, and her body began to feel the wild swells of orgasm. She could hear her own moaning filling the stable....

With a sudden directness, a long talon of leather seized Liza about the waist. The horsewhip in Oliver's hand reached out and insured his dominion over her. His message was clearly understood by all: Time to take the focus off Liza and see to Hilary.

"Tie her to the pillar," Oliver directed.

And then Oliver turned to Diana, his head motioning toward Hilary. "You were the injured party this afternoon," he said. "The bitch is yours to take since she refused to take you."

The night was like a wild vision taken directly from many of Hilary's past fantasies. The erotic dance of her mistress, the cat winding around her body; Oliver tearing the fulfillment away from her, forcing the drama in another direction. It was a scene far removed from the quiet sensuality of Hilary's first encounter in the morning room, the day that she had sealed her fate to become part of this drama.

Hilary realized that she had entered a world where she had no control, and this realization gave her indescribable pleasure.

And then it was Diana's turn to approach her. Hilary watched with dread as the fierce woman picked up the abandoned cat-o'-nine-tails from the hay-strewn floor of the stable. She let it drag beside her as she waltzed her way toward the slave. Every step she took mocked Hilary's submission. Diana was corseted in leather, her plain black bustier barely supporting her voluptuous breasts. Her heels were high like Liza's, but she wore leather boots that rose up long legs to her crotch. The boots glistened in the dim candlelight of the stable.

She stroked Hilary's chin with her finger, her long nails clawing at her neck. "It's time that you paid," she said, smiling in such a way that Hilary cringed despite herself.

Diana took her time. She slowly ran her eyes and her hands and the end of the cat over Hilary's pulsating body. She looked wild and feral, as though any moment she would maul the young woman, devour

The Applicant

her, take her brutally. Diana was ready to make Hilary pay for her dreadful oversight that afternoon.

But Diana turned. She had other debts to square before she dove into the delectable flesh of the new submissive. She focused her frightening presence on the mistress of the estate. Liza was breathing hard, her eyes closed, her head back, lost in her own world.

"Miss Liza," Diana said sarcastically, squaring her hips in front of the woman. "You will watch. Is that clear?"

Hilary watched as Liza looked to Oliver where he sat casually in the corner of the tack room. He seemed unconcerned with Liza's plight. She looked to him for mercy, but he was indifferent.

Diana slapped Liza's face hard. Hilary winced as her mistress did.

"Have I made myself clear?"

Liza's nostrils flared. Hilary sensed Liza's desire to strike back, and her fury at the binding that prevented her from taking control.

"Yes, you have," she finally replied.

Diana gloated, apparently satisfied with Liza's defiant tone. Diana gazed at Liza thoughtfully. "I'd truly forgotten how lovely it is to have you under my control. It brings back the most delicious memories."

Liza looked away, but Diana grabbed her face and forced their eyes to meet. Diana let loose a screaming laugh and then let Liza's face go, turning her full attention to Hilary.

"Now, my little one," she said, unfastening the bonds behind the sweet submissive, "let's see *you* dance." She shoved Hilary to the center of the stable floor, and Hilary nearly fell. She froze with fear.

"You'd better dance, or this is going to be an extremely painful night for you." Diana cracked the cat-o'-nine-tails to give meaning to her threat. The

195

eight strands of leather hit Hilary's back and the front of her thighs. The strands curled around her, cutting into her flesh. She jumped from the jolt of pain. It was hard to think of dancing when her main focus was on dodging another blow. Unlike the blows administered by Mistress Liza, these did not give Hilary pleasure.

"Dance," Diana ordered. And with strokes of lesser force, Diana wielded the cat against the woman's body again. Pink stripes were beginning to appear on Hilary's flesh where the whip had landed, but these blows did not give her the same sensation of shock and pain as the first did. Hilary was surprised to find that they were stimulating and they aroused the sex heat in her immediately. Still, she was unable to dance; fear and self-consciousness were preventing her. It would be impossible for Hilary to imitate her mistress.

She was nearly in tears, and she tried to hold them back. Suddenly she wanted nothing more than to let them flow; she wanted to release her fear and frustration.

"I can do nothing more with her," Diana announced. She turned to Oliver, whose dispassionate pose was unaltered by the recent unfolding of events.

"Do you wish to walk away unfulfilled? Do you wish to disappoint your mistress?" he asked Hilary, sounding like a calm, yet authoritative schoolmaster. He stood and yanked her close to him, pulling her chin up so that they stood face to face. "Do you wish to give her up for a moment's weakness?"

Hilary stood in silence, not knowing what to do or say.

"Tell us now, so that we can proceed. Of course we are at your beck and call." His words mocked her.

The Applicant

Hilary shivered with unrequited passion and desire. Her heart leapt to realize that she was worthy enough to merit a second chance. She wanted nothing more than to belong to both him and Liza. She knew that she had to complete the night's rituals, no matter how frightened she was.

"I apologize to you and to my mistress, Liza. I apologize to Diana for not fulfilling my task. I put myself in your hands and beg for another chance."

Oliver stared at her. She was a true submissive, but she had a fire burning inside. She was a lot like Liza in that way.

"Sometimes, my dear, one must do what one fears most in order to have what is most desired." He picked up the cat from the stable floor and wrapped the long tails around Hilary's neck, letting the ends dangle down the back of her body. He pulled the strands tight to emphasize his point. And then he removed the whip and handed it to Diana.

"You may begin from the beginning, Diana."

Diana smiled at him, delighted that she could again begin to administer her delicious torments to such a succulent piece of young and willing flesh. Oliver returned to his place in the corner of the tack room.

"Use your tongue on me," Diana commanded. "Start with your lips."

It seemed a fair consolation to Hilary, and she could comply with the order. Glimpsing Liza in the corner restored Hilary's strength, and she felt grateful for the opportunity to resume. Hilary's lips met Diana's in a kiss. She licked them until they parted to receive her tongue. And then Hilary kissed Diana's neck. She worked slowly and sensually, beginning to take pleasure in the woman's soft, pliant flesh. She played with her, giving in to the lust that was fueled by rage. Hilary let her lips slowly caress Diana's cleavage, and then with her hands she released the redhead's large breasts from the corset and began furiously to suck and bite her nipples. She relished the feel of the delicate buds on the tip of her tongue, and the feel of the warm soft flesh about the nipple yielded to her mouth. She felt all the eyes of the audience upon her, and this exhibitionism turned her on, pressed her to be more deliberate and wild with her tongue. Diana moaned, obviously enjoying the wonderful sensations given her by Hilary's deft tongue, lips, and teeth. Slowly, Hilary worked her way toward Diana's pussy. She saw the moist red hair, and her own cunt pulsed with longing.

"My ass first," Diana said in a low voice, and she turned to offer Hilary her pink, tightly puckered anus. Diana bent over a bale of hay, and said in a hoarse voice, "Take it all." She reached around, grabbed her ass cheeks, and spread her crack wide open, exposing her ass and cunt to Hilary's searching mouth.

Hilary knelt to obey. She slowly tongued Diana's crack; then she rimmed her asshole, and slyly inserted her tongue into its opening. She moved down to the succulent pussy and her tongue found the folds of hot, wet, and ready flesh. Hilary moved her tongue back to Diana's asshole, and she flicked it around the edges of the tightly puckered hole. Diana's hips began to gyrate with pleasure, as Hilary continued to rim her expertly. Hilary was on fire; she was taking great pleasure in eating this fierce woman. She revisited Diana's pussy and began to suck hungrily on her clit. Knowing that Liza and Oliver were watching made Hilary's desire all the more potent, and that led her to even more passionate kisses on Diana's cunt.

Diana rolled over to display her cunt fully to

The Applicant

Hilary's attention. She wanted her passions met hard and fast. Her hands kept her cunt exposed and accessible. Liza and Oliver watched as Hilary's mouth devoured the pouty, pink pussy, eating Diana out as if she were a full-course meal.

"Suck me hard!" Diana breathed. And as she said this, she began to spank Hilary's ass as Hilary writhed over her, fucking her with her tongue. The harder her hand fell on Hilary's flesh, the deeper the young woman pushed her tongue into Diana's cunt. Their bodies were moving in heated unison. The scent of steamed, wet pussies filled the air.

It was punishment for Liza to watch. It was anguish to see the woman she desired servicing the bitch she hated. It was torture to see Hilary enjoying her task. Hilary's body writhed seductively in front of Liza, and the older woman was helpless to reach out and take what was rightfully hers. She felt humiliated and bested by Diana in Oliver's presence. She wanted to scream.

Hilary sucked Diana hard and Diana continued to smack her ass. They were riding out a rhythm that could not be stopped. Hilary was overcome, her body moving forward to greet the whip and Diana's gleaming, dripping-wet pussy. Diana pushed her hips hard into Hilary's face, bucking strongly against her tongue, smashing her cunt into Hilary's hungry mouth. She thrust again and again in a steady beat until her orgasm was drawn out of her body, and she collapsed back in breathless release.

Without missing a beat, Oliver rose and crossed the room to where Hilary sat back on her knees, her face red with exertion. Liza watched the three of them in the center of the room, and tears fell recklessly down her face. She watched as Oliver helped Hilary stand. She watched as, holding tightly to

Hilary, he leaned down and gave Diana a long passionate kiss. And then she watched as Oliver took Hilary from the stable without so much as a glance in her direction. Although the unfolding events were no surprise to the well-trained lady of the house, the images brought a heaviness to her heart. On one level, it was her husband she craved attention from; yet on another, perhaps more serene level, it was the woman he was about to fuck that Liza wanted.

CHAPTER XV

Fifteen

Hilary was still on fire. She had once more been close to falling over the edge into an abyss of pleasure and had been denied. She was pulled along in great haste by Oliver. She felt as if the whole night had been part of a long waking dream, and she could not decide yet if it was a nightmare or sweet fantasy.

His strides were long and swift, making it difficult for her to keep up with him. Suddenly, he stopped and pushed her roughly to the ground at his feet. He stood over her, just looking at her for a moment, and then he opened his riding breeches to reveal his handsome cock; it was engorged with passion. He pulled her up roughly to his groin by her shoulders and forced himself into her mouth. She barely had time to open for him when his cock pressed inward.

She was so startled by the suddenness of his movement, she didn't gulp for air or gag. She simply took him—all of him. He plowed himself in and out, back and forth, pushing deep into her throat until he screamed out into the night, letting his hot come flow directly down her willing throat. His yell of pleasure rose into the air like a wild animal cry that seemed to rattle the trees and move the clouds. It was like the howl of a thing not quite human.

The lustful sound of Oliver's orgasmic expression cut through the other cries of pleasure that were coming from the bodies that fucked, sucked, and writhed on the floor of the stable. It seemed as if everyone stopped in their passionate fucking to acknowledge the sex scream of the master of the estate; that same cry cut Liza to the bone. She heard his scream as it penetrated the night, and she knew that Oliver wanted her to be aware of his satisfaction. And then, as quickly as it had become silent, the orgy in the stable resumed its hot, happy, joyous pace. Liza was further tortured by having to witness her guest's pleasure without being allowed to partake at all. She felt miserably alone.

She didn't want to think. She only wanted to sleep and to hide from the reality of the day's wild happenings. She wanted to escape into the safer realms of night and forget her humiliation.

Suddenly Liza felt Diana's breath right on her face; she was practically touching her, she stood so close.

"I hope you enjoyed yourself this evening, Liza dear," she said with mocking elegance. "I certainly did."

With that, the vengeful, voluptuous bitch stepped back and spread her cunt lips wide apart, exposing her still-gleaming, wet pussy, and began to mastur-

The Applicant

bate herself in front of Liza, whose own hands were not allowed contact with even her own body on this night.

Liza watched as Diana manipulated her juicy twat, finger-fucking herself, rubbing around her asshole, and ultimately, bringing her middle finger to the hot, hard clit bud and furiously massaging the sweet pink meat until an orgasm was inevitable.

Liza watched, spellbound, her own cunt welling with heat despite her disdain for Diana. Her poor, wet, swollen cunt was so ferociously turned on, she would have liked to feel even Diana's vile mouth hungrily suck out some of her boiling sex syrup.

Even though it was against the rules, Liza could not help rocking back and forth and manipulating the weight of her crotch so as to create friction on her clit, hoping she could rock herself into an orgasm. Her face became tense, as she focused all her energy on her pussy; her eyes were on Diana all the while.

Then, just as she felt she might get off, Diana's face grew tight with passion. Her body emitted a dense, musky perfume, and the muscles of her cunt began to twitch as her finger worked diligently on her clit, which was about to explode like a rocket leaving a launch pad.

Just as the juice of her self-expression came pouring forth, Diana smiled at her audience of one. And Liza, nearly exhausted from her unfulfilled desires, could only stare, feeling powerless.

Diana, now complete, dipped that same finger into the well of her desires and brought the wetness to Liza's lips. She rubbed her cunt juice along the lower lip and slipped the finger into the poor woman's mouth.

"You might as well lick it," Diana said, a wicked grin on her face. "It's all you'll be getting tonight."

With her cunt on fire and her heart sinking with sadness, Liza did as she was told and sucked the juice fully from Diana's fingers, adding to her frustration and humiliation.

Then she left for the sanctum of her own bed.

At last darkness enveloped her. It was cold and lonely in her room and her body ached, but that seemed to be the least of her concerns.

Finally, toward dawn, *he* entered the room, silent as always.

She waited for a word, but he said nothing. Her courage grew and then waned, but her rage was constant. Fear and jealousy welled up within her.

She watched him sit down wearily in the chair and tug at his riding boots.

"Come help me get these off, Liza," he said at last.

His voice was nonchalant, as though nothing had transpired except a midnight ride on his horse.

She didn't move, and after a moment he looked up. She looked as well, her gaze trying to burn him.

"You've humiliated me in front of my friends," she exploded at last. "How could you do that to me?" She leapt off the bed and flew at him, the full force of her fury brewing to the surface.

"If you don't want me anymore, tell me right now and I will leave immediately."

He stared at her with wonder, looking as though he were about to laugh.

"I hate you," she screamed. "I thought you loved me. I hate you ... how could you ..." She glared at him, tears beginning to run down her cheeks.

She turned away from him and faced the windows, ashamed of her outburst and what she'd already said. She looked out at the lawn of the estate and suddenly felt as though she were in a foreign land.

The Applicant

"You don't care, do you?" she said, not risking the shame of seeing his laughing eyes again. She was tired, and her anger had left her suddenly weary. There was a long gap of silence during which Liza sagged to the floor as though she were pressed there by an unbelievable burden.

"Elizabeth," he said at last.

"Don't call me that. Don't ..."

"Elizabeth," he said again, his voice rising above hers. "Come here," he said and grabbed her wrists, pulling her firmly to the bed.

"No, No!" she shouted, shaking herself free from his grasp.

They stared at each other for a long time, locked in a silent battle. His face betrayed no emotion. And then rather suddenly, he burst into laughter. It was a full sound that rang throughout the bedroom. His laugh was not mocking or cruel, but full of joy. Liza stared at him in disbelief. Her rage and torment were washed away in the sound of his laugh.

He pulled her to the bed, tearing away the curtains that clothed the heavy canopy of their inner sanctum. He sat her down beside him, his hand gently resting on her thigh.

"Elizabeth my dear, what about this weekend didn't you like?"

It was a rhetorical question, and he proceeded. "You loved the drama, the tears, and the raging. You loved being assaulted by Stephen. You loved to dance beautifully before an audience. You reveled in your humiliation."

He paused and looked at her a long while and then said again, "Now tell me, what didn't you like about this weekend?"

She couldn't answer. She sat and cried silently.

"You're right, my darling," she said at last. "I did. I loved it all."

"Of course."

He smiled and pulled Liza to him. His mouth covered hers in a deep kiss, his tongue playing lightly with hers. He laid her back on the bed, the soft down of the pillows and comforters taking them in. His hands gently roved her body, and her hands began to hungrily strip away his clothing. At last, he was naked and their bodies were touching. Their lovemaking began slowly and deliberately.

She opened herself wide as he brought the head of his hard cock to the opening of her awaiting cunt, and he pressed himself home on the first thrust. He sucked and bit her nipples as he battered her deliciously with his lust, and she writhed beneath, pressing her hips against his groin, so as to receive it all, so as to leave nothing untasted. They fucked in the sensual rhythm that was all their own—the one that would never and could never belong to anyone but these two, who moved together in passion as one.

Any questions that Liza had about his feelings for her were dispelled instantly. She dug her fingers into his loins and pulled him in deeper. He responded with a force that made their bodies come together in a relentless fever. He seemed to thrust in and out of her for hours, holding back his passion juice. Liza finally burst, her wetness coming down all over her husband's hard cock. Even then, he just kept fucking her until she came again and again and ...

It was hours into the night before they rested. Never had Liza been more satisfied.

Before he fell asleep, he whispered. "Elizabeth, you alone know me."

The guests milled about the grounds in the morning

The Applicant

hours, enjoying the lovely day. Neither their host, hostess or their delightful new addition appeared during the morning. Yet everyone knew that they had been present at a gathering that would be discussed for years to come. They all felt satisfied.

Hilary lay in her small room, alone. She was ultimately confused by the tiring day and night that preceded the morning sun.

She was wide awake as soon as the light broke through the window of the attic. The feelings of the previous evening still haunted her. She wondered if the events she'd experienced were dreams; they were events that seemed to be more dreamlike than real, though she was almost certain they had actually happened.

She lay on the bed and wondered if she had just been used as a pawn, an intricate player in *Liza's* training. There were many moments in the previous evening when Liza seemed as surprised by the turn of events as Hilary was herself.

Oliver was the only one who ruled the estate, and what a ruler he was. He fucked with an electricity that seemed to charge every room. Thoughts of Oliver, his big cock and commanding ways, made her body come alive instantly. She wanted him. She wanted him to take her again and again. She wondered if she secretly desired to take Liza's place in his bed, or did she want to share it? Was either of those fantasies an option? Had she passed the test?

Hilary stayed there, confused thoughts and feelings buzzing through her head, while her sexuality warmed up like a microwave oven. As strange as it all seemed, as strange as it all was, Hilary wanted more—she wanted it all.

The guests lounged by the pool eating and drinking,

enjoying the afternoon sun. Finally, Oliver and Liza made themselves present. Elegant and graceful, they stood together on the terrace, well aware of the fact that they made a handsome pair. They were the perfect match of light and dark, submissive and dominant. Liza was confident of the fact that she was mistress to his mastery.

Her gaze fell upon Diana, the woman who had trained her so well. She smiled to herself, realizing that she could accept Diana as a willing player in their complicated little game. She knew ultimately that Diana's passion and heat only made the game that much more exciting. Knowing this gave Liza a sense of power, and she felt victorious over Diana for the first time since she had known her.

Diana saw Liza looking at her and she approached the stunning couple. "I've trained you well," she said.

Liza smiled with delight. For even as much as she detested Diana, she secretly wanted her approval.

Liza attended to her other guests graciously, and then she returned to the house, allowing Oliver to finish with the formal good-byes. There was one more thing to attend to before the drama was at its final scene.

CHAPTER XVI

Sixteen

The stairs creaked as he mounted them. He could smell the scent of rosewood in the thick air, and he felt the pressure of a single-minded thought that was manifesting itself in his crotch. He was going to take her, no matter what.

He withdrew the key from his pocket and inserted it into the old lock. He swung open the door and found himself face to face with Hilary. She looked frightened. That pleased him.

Without pausing for a moment, Stephen reached forward, and was about to grab her hair when he was halted by Oliver's voice.

"She is not yours to take. Put the collar on her and bring her down."

Stephen didn't turn to face his master. He let go of

Hilary and silently obeyed the command. He knew that if he breached his contract, he would be expelled from the estate immediately; he wasn't about to ruin a good thing. Not just for a taste of pussy; not just for a fuck with the new submissive.

"Yes, sir," he said.

Oliver retreated silently. No one ever questioned or disobeyed the master of the house—no one who wanted to stay and play.

She paused at the bedroom door as Stephen swung it open for her. All the waiting, all the games and all the submissions were a prelude to what was beyond the door. She was exhilarated to find herself at last at the end of her long wait. He ushered her through the door and then quietly left, so that she could discover what fulfillment truly meant.

The room was dark, and in the cozy chamber it seemed as if time were suspended. A single candle burned, giving off a soft glow; it cast heavy shadows on the walls. The room seemed magic. Hilary could see a male figure moving toward her. It was Oliver.

"Come sit, my dear," he said, motioning to a chair. "You look lovely."

She sat, humbled by the tenderness in his voice and the quiet in the room.

"Do you understand what you are giving yourself to, Hilary?" he asked her. "Do you understand that you are caught in a complicated web of pleasure and pain, and that here there will always be someone to challenge your limits? On this path that you've chosen there will always be assaults on the strength and character of your endurance. I want you to understand that this path has no limitations, and that no one can stop your progress except you." He spoke with a soft yet searing intensity.

The Applicant

"I do," she replied

He laughed a little. "No. You don't understand at all. But it is enough for you to know that you wish to proceed in our world. Every day that you stay here, more will be expected of you. Do you understand that?"

"I think so," she replied hesitantly.

"When you cease to enjoy yourself, it is time for you to leave. Do you understand?"

"Yes," she said with certainty.

"Good," he replied.

He looked into her eyes for a long moment. She felt consumed by him, as if he were taking her. It seemed that he knew her in ways that she didn't even know herself, and she realized that was why she was here. She was here to understand herself more deeply. Oliver held a key that he would someday turn over to her, so she could unlock her own doors and understand the mysteries.

He went to an armoire that stood against the wall and pulled from it a mass of rope and leather. He tossed the tangled mass to a corner of the room. Hilary suddenly noticed the shadow of Liza moving out of the darkness.

"Take her," he commanded, and he withdrew to the shadows as his wife took over the moment and claimed Hilary.

Liza wore a leather corset and boots that climbed all the way up her perfect thighs. Her hair was like a lion's mane, and her eyes were painted a smouldering dark color. Hilary braced herself for the moment she had been waiting for so impatiently.

With ropes and leathers in hand, Liza grasped Hilary's arms and pulled her to the bed. She pushed Hilary down on the mattress and swiftly tied her wrists to the bedpost and her ankles to the footboard.

Hilary's legs were spread so very wide that her pink, swelling cunt lips were visible, and the scent of sex wafted up from between her legs. She watched, her eyelids half closed with desire, as Liza reached to a table and strapped on a heavy leather belt which supported a big, heavy dildo. Liza's body was suddenly transformed from a soft feminine form to an aggressive masculine body.

The dildo was made of a flesh-colored rubber, with a skin-soft outer layer and a thick, erect inner tube. It was big and hard, and Hilary's cunt filled with juice when she saw her mistress cover her bare, cleanshaven pussy with the ten-inch male protrusion. The dildo had an apparatus that, when strapped, served as a clit-rubber as well as a cunt-fucker. The harder she'd thrust, the more her clit would get slammed by the fat, hard piece of rubber. The warm anticipation made both pussies hot and wet. Hilary lifted her hips, begging for the first satisfying thrust from her mistress.

Liza stood before her for a moment longer. She came closer and closer to Hilary, and her eyes fixed on the young woman with the same deep intensity that the slave had seen in Oliver. Then Liza moved in to claim Hilary's body.

Liza slid her trim body between Hilary's wide-open legs. She studied the succulent cunt before her—the pouty, pink lips, even more swollen with lust, the fat folds that lazily covered the sweet pink opening. With a thumb and forefinger she parted Hilary's cunt fully and looked into the sweet opening. Bending her head, she sniffed the female scent and blew a soft sigh into the opening, tingling her captive with a gentle female breath while preparing her for a big, hard cock. Still holding Hilary's hole apart, Liza used a middle finger to gently prod the opening fur-

The Applicant

ther. She slipped the finger in her mouth and wet it first, then slipped it into Hilary's cunt. It was hot and wet inside, and just the soft touch of Liza's finger made Hilary press up for more. Adding one more finger, Liza filled the gaping opening briefly with two fingers, rubbing them in and out, back and forth, to create a delicious friction. Next, the fingers were withdrawn and the hand became a fist. Liza knuckle-fucked the swelling cunt opening until she could work the whole fist inward, giving Hilary just a taste of what was to come.

Resonant groans escaped from Hilary. She could not control them, and her hips writhed back and forth in unison with Liza's fist. For the first time in her life, Hilary was getting fist-fucked. She could feel the balled-up fingers pressing against her female organs and was conscious of Liza's wrist stretching her cunt opening wider. It hurt, but it was so pleasurable; it felt like she was being ripped open, but she wanted more. She virtually impaled herself on her mistress' fist. Liza moved slowly, deliberately; Hilary's hips moved frantically, begging for more.

Liza's hand was wet with pussy juice. Her own cunt was sweating and dripping from the passion that stirred between the two women. Liza rubbed the fake cock against Hilary's leg, pressing the rubber against her own swelling clit. She was ready to fuck her wonderful, obedient submissive. Again, there would have to be pleasure and pain at once.

"Tighten your cunt muscles," Liza commanded. Hilary obeyed, squeezing her wet opening so that the muscles closed tight like an anus. "Keep it tight," Liza said.

She took some lubricant and rubbed it on her dildo, which, atop her swelling clit bud, felt like it was getting heavier and more erect. She also oiled the rim of Hilary's clenched cunt. She mounted her and pressed the cock to the opening. "Stay tight," she said. "Fight it until I tell you to surrender."

A thrill rose in Hilary's cunt, flowing through her anus and up to her tits. Once again, she was being denied what she wanted so much. She obeyed, keeping her cunt closed as her mistress nudged the huge cockhead into her opening. She fought it with clenching cunt muscles, but she fought her own impulse to open and receive even harder. She wanted to take all of it, fully, deeply, deliciously.

Liza's clit was getting a free ride from the tension created by Hilary's closed muscles. She began to push, to shove, to pound the false cock into her woman. Hilary continued to keep herself closed until Liza finally forced her way in with one big, powerful thrust.

"Open, now," Liza demanded, feeling the big cock slide into the waiting cunt. "Open wide, take me."

Hilary released her cunt muscles, and the dildo immediately slammed home, filling her dripping-wet, horny hole with the fullness she so desired. Liza fucked her like a man would fuck his woman. And she shoved that big dildo up as far as it would go. Using her hip power, she pulled it all the way out and shoved it back in.

Hilary was wild with passion, her body on fire. She was whimpering, begging, gyrating beyond control, trying to get more than the ten inches inside her; trying to get Liza inside her. The straps pulled painfully on her arms and legs as she tried to move her essentially immovable body to greet Liza's thrusts. Liza was also swept away on a pleasure wave, her cunt twitching behind the dildo, her clit rubbing wildly into the back of the rubber. She felt like the cock was real, like she was fucking Hilary with her very own, real cock.

The Applicant

Liza felt totally powerful and knew, in that moment, what a great power men feel when they shove their hard cocks into waiting cunts. Her pussy-cock felt like it would explode; she pressed deeper into Hilary and leaned hard against her body. She loved the feel of a woman writhing beneath her. And Hilary loved the feel of a woman writhing atop her. This ten-inch cock was the largest and fattest Hilary had ever known; it tore at her cunt as it pierced her. It was only fitting that her mistress would be capable of violating her so thoroughly.

The two women moaned in unison. Liza pushed deeper and deeper, harder and harder, and a light-headed feeling took over. Her cunt was all atingle. As she fucked her sweet submissive, she brought her breasts down on Hilary's. Their titties touched flesh to flesh; their nipples kissed.

Liza began to kiss Hilary on the mouth, to suck on the sweet tongue hungrily and fully devour her lover with macho, aggressive French kisses. She ran her mouth around her lover's parted lips, kissing her with passion as Hilary responded in kind, giving her mistress her own tongue while sucking Liza's as well.

The two were very aware of their rubbing titties, each with nipples so erect that they were like little rocks; the pleasure shot right down to their gyrating pussies, both on the edge of exploding yet reserving the ultimate release for a moment in the future— until Hilary could stand it no more. The sweet, submissive, obedient Hilary, denied Liza's touch for so long, begged for her mistress to bring her to orgasm, and to join her in the wet explosion. Hilary's cunt was on the verge of a wild spurt of wetness; her breath quickened, and her cunt muscles twitched and clenched and were ready to explode. Liza, sensing this nearness, suddenly pulled out of Hilary's fluttering pussy.

"No, no, please," Hilary begged, her now-empty cunt gaping, clenching at the air. "Please, please, take me and let me give you my juice. Please take my juice from me." The tingle in her clit was alive. Just one touch, one kiss would do it.

Her wrists and legs were suddenly untied. She was quickly turned around and her weakened knees were hoisted until she was in a kneeling position. Before she even knew what was happening, his large, male hands were hungrily, deliberately spreading her asshole wide apart, and a fat tongue was rimming her, licking her, wetting her in a delicious way. The tongue pressed inward and pulled out of her ass; it pushed in and pulled out, until Hilary was beyond any recognition of what part of her body the pleasure was actually coming from.

Oliver had stood and watched the two cunts have their wild fuck. He waited, as always, till the most suspenseful moment to step in and play. The ultimate was about to happen: Hilary, Liza, and Oliver would become as one.

Liza yanked the dildo strap from her waist and pulled the rubber cock from her burning, swelling cunt. She quickly arranged her body so that her pussy was right on the lips of her sweet sex slave. She positioned her head just under Hilary's raised hips. She waited until she could tell Oliver was ready.

He had tongued Hilary's asshole so deliciously that it was totally wet. He put lubricant on his hard, swollen cock and positioned it at the still-tight entrance. Just as he pressed home, filling her asshole up with his big, hard, *real* cock, Liza's mouth rose to greet Hilary's raised cunt. She licked the lips slowly and spread the pussy-hole open with her fingers, slowly finger-fucking the young woman with two, then three long fingers. Then, with the thumb and

The Applicant

forefinger of each hand, she pulled on Hilary's fat cunt lips, tugged them apart and downward, and brought the sweet, hot, hard love bud to her lips. She kissed, she slurped, she sucked, just as Oliver fully penetrated Hilary's anus with his cock.

Hilary nearly lost her breath, but dove her mouth into Liza's waiting, wanting, hungry pussy; she ate her mistress out, licking the woman's cunt hole clean with her hot tongue. But she was crazed with the heat of passion. Oliver was fucking her so hard, filling her so deeply, and Liza was sucking her so intensely, that Hilary was all on fire. Liza was sucking out the cunt juice; Oliver was fucking it out from the other end. Her asshole was tearing, and yet it was filled with pleasure; her clit was all tingly and sensitive, yet afire with ecstasy. She shoved her cunt into Liza's mouth and pressed her ass into Oliver's groin.

Sensing the wildfire running through her slave, Liza pushed her pussy into Hilary's mouth and rubbed it against the sweet lips, pushing it against the teeth, slamming it into her female lover. Hilary was wild, and licked at Liza like an animal, with no rhyme or reason, but in a way that lifted the love bud into an even higher state, close to exploding.

Liza kept at Hilary's clit, sucking it wildly while pulling apart the skin, making it totally exposed, until Hilary began to really buck, to go wild, to spill herself into her mistress' mouth. Liza rubbed herself more furiously, face-fucking her slave while her husband's hard cock slammed into his favorite place—the nice, tight ass. Oliver's passion began to boil beyond control, and he suddenly jerked the smooth ass cheeks as far apart as possible as he plowed into Hilary to the hilt. She flinched, and her cunt went even deeper into Liza's mouth. Her orgasm was right there and Liza got it, sucking it out with a flickering tongue and a vibrating motion of her mouth.

Oliver screamed that wild, animal cry as he poured his hot jism into Hilary's anal opening; and Hilary screamed out as Liza sucked out the last of her dripping juices. As Hilary cried out her pleasure, Liza forced her whole clit and upper pussy-lips into the young woman's mouth. Her ass still stuffed with Oliver's huge cock, and her pussy atingle with orgasmic contractions, Hilary focused her last bit of energy onto Liza's beautiful pussy, changing her frenzied pace to a slower, measured, sucking motion. Now it was Liza who groaned and moaned and begged to be sucked off. And she was, deliciously, by the mouth she had come to desire more than any other. She was relaxed as her cunt erupted into a sweet orgasm. Hilary sucked her until every last cunt contraction was complete. Then she licked the sweet juice from Liza's delicious pussy. Oliver, composed now after the explosion that was sucked from him by Hilary's excitingly tight ass, watched while his wife groaned and quivered with joy as her cunt spat out the pent-up orgasm.

Then Oliver, smiling down on both women, removed himself from Hilary and from the room. Without a word, he was gone. Liza didn't know where he was off to; she didn't care. She was left alone with Hilary. There were no tests, no training, no demands. Just the two of them, together. The two women were finally collecting their prizes—one another!

The two women rested, lying arm in arm with legs entwined, and they slept for a sweet while in the afternoon. When they awoke, they lay there for a time, enjoying each other's warmth.

Finally, Hilary luxuriously stretched her long legs

and rose from the bed. She crossed the room and stood by the window, staring out at the late-afternoon shadows that stretched across the lawn. Liza admired her from the bed. The incredible beauty of her slave was reigniting the fires in her body.

"Dance for me," Liza requested.

This time Hilary did not give in to fear or feel embarrassed. She twirled and swirled and danced sensually for Liza's eyes only, gyrating her hips, sexily lifting her legs to expose her pussy. She was touching her nipples, squeezing and jiggling her titties. She lost herself in an array of impromptu motions, each move offering her mistress-lover a better, deeper, closer view of her sexual anatomy. Hilary danced around Liza, teasingly pushing her tits into Liza's face. Then, in a burst of improvisational sexual theater and a true show of released inhibition, she bent over, spreading her ass cheeks wide and showing her tight, pink, slightly-irritated asshole to her mistress. She stood close to Liza, so the view was good. And Liza looked in awe at the place her husband so adored fucking, a place her husband had filled with so many different things—cock, dildo, finger, tongue. Hilary swished her hips flirtatiously, offering the shrine of Oliver's affections to her lover. She didn't even understand why she was doing it, or what moved her. And she stopped only when she was summoned to the bed.

Liza's pussy was starting to boil again. Her mouth, her tits, her cunt, and her own ass filled with longing. She was intrigued by the prospect of understanding Oliver's lust for Hilary and wanted to know his anal attraction intimately. She wanted to be Oliver and rip into Hilary's asshole; first, she would play.

"Bend over my lap, darling," Liza said.

Hilary obeyed gleefully. She playfully straddled

Liza, laying her ass across the woman's lap in such a way that their two hairless pussies were touching.

"Let me see what Oliver loves here," Liza said, gently spreading open Hilary's ass. It was still red and sore from being fucked by the master. As was the custom when fucked by Oliver, Hilary had not cleaned herself. Although Oliver always liked to begin with a clean, sweet-smelling asshole, what Oliver left behind was a good omen, and the combined aroma of jism and ass left a strong animal scent that recalled the lust that had visited there.

Liza pushed a finger toward the asshole and past the rim; Hilary flinched and then relaxed. Liza's finger went deeper, the passage oiled by Oliver's come. She pressed the finger in deep, till she could go no further, till her knuckle nearly disappeared. Then she moved the finger back and forth and finger-fucked Hilary until the woman was past the pain. Liza shoved two fingers in next. Although Hilary could feel the soreness, it became a delicious stretching feeling that surrounded the building fullness. Her cunt was beginning to swell, the heat in her sex meat totally obliterating the feeling of rawness.

Just as Hilary began to move rhythmically along with Liza's fingers, Liza grabbed hold of one of the leather straps that had bound her slave before. She slapped Hilary hard, then softly, then softly and hard again, until Hilary writhed wildly. She changed the pattern so Hilary never knew what kind of slap to expect. She made delicious pink marks across Hilary's butt flesh. Then she told her sweet submissive to kneel on all fours. Hilary did, and again took the receptive position that Oliver had trained her for. She awaited her lover's next move with anticipation.

Liza got behind Hilary and, without hesitation, ate out her asshole, cleaning it of Oliver's come and

The Applicant

Oliver's presence. She began by spreading the pink opening just wide enough that the sore part could be stretched and the opening could be pleasured with her hot, wet, probing tongue. She sucked on the puckered anus, and licked and sniffed at the warm scent of what her husband had left behind and what he had brought to the surface; she rubbed her face in it. She wanted every part of it, every morsel. The odor collected on her cheeks, her nose; she rubbed into it to get more. She was growing still more lustful and hungry and plunged her tongue in deep. Hilary moaned, groaned, and pressed her ass up for more as Liza dug deeper, now using her teeth to nibble and bite her way into the opening. Hilary felt herself spreading gently. The soreness lifted and was replaced by a different pain. Liza was gnawing at Hilary's ass, as if trying to bite out a bigger hole. The teeth scratched the surface; they chewed at the puckered rim and dove into the inner sanctum.

"Ah, Liza, yes, eat me like that," Hilary was groaning, almost out of breath, wild with a renewed passion. "Oh Liza, please, take it, yes, take it all. Rip me open like ... Oliver."

There, she'd said it. She wanted her mistress to fuck her the way her master did. And her mistress wanted the same.

Liza strapped the dildo on again, pressing it tight against her own swollen cunt lips and erect clitoris. She straddled Hilary from behind. Grabbing hold of the dildo and guiding it with her hand, she dipped the rubber hard-on into Hilary's wet cunt, to tease and taunt; to make Hilary beg.

"Tell me what you want," Liza whispered breathlessly in Hilary's ear, punctuating it by rimming the lobe and then plunging her tongue into the ear canal.

"Tell me how you want to be fucked by Oliver. Talk to me like I'm Oliver."

And for a moment in time, Liza became her husband. There was no telling wife from husband, for each was as powerful. Each had a cock and could fuck ass with it.

"Fuck me, like you did before," Hilary panted. "My asshole is yours, Oliver. You are the master of my ass."

"That's right," Liza said, becoming Oliver as she did. "This is mine and mine alone. I can take it any time. I can take it now, you bitch. I'm going to take it. Open up. Open this asshole good and wide."

Liza put a slab of lubricant on her cock and plunged the dildo into the sweet ass before her. She plunged hard and went deep on the first thrust. She plunged right past the soreness that Oliver had left behind. The tears welled in Hilary's eyes as the ten-inch cock filled her asshole. It was bigger than Oliver, and it stretched her wider and further than anything she'd ever felt. Yet for every twinge of pain her ass endured, her pussy swelled and sent a message to her pleasure center—to keep going, to take more.

Liza fucked hard and deep and fast, and she ripped Hilary as she did. It hurt. Liza knew it must, but she couldn't stop; she had to take it all. She had to come in Hilary's ass.

Hilary wanted Liza to explode, too. She pressed her ass up to greet Liza's thrusts; she wanted that ten-inch cock deep inside. She wanted to explode while Liza ripped into her.

"Touch your clit and make it come," Liza panted. "Make that pussy come with me ... come on, get it ready."

Liza's own clit was on fire. Rubbing furiously against the rubber on the pussy side of the dildo, she

The Applicant

knew she was going to get off soon; she felt her cunt exploding like a cock in her girl lover's asshole. She felt herself exploding the way Oliver had. Fully immersed inside his favorite place, he was powerful as he fucked. He was powerful as he came. He was powerful as he took a woman in the ass like an animal and then howled like a wolf.

"I am fucking you with my cock," Liza was saying, panting, shaking. "I am fucking your submissive ass with my big cock. I am hurting you and giving you pleasure all at once. I'm fucking you, fucking you, fuck ... ing ... you."

With one powerful push of the hips, Liza plowed her cock in to the hilt and rubbed, rubbed, rubbed against it until her clit exploded and her orgasm began. Slowly at first, it picked up speed and got bigger and bigger until her whole body felt the effects of her contracting womb; she came in Hilary's asshole.

At the same moment, Hilary's momentum picked up speed and she was playing furiously with her own pussy. Her clit, now hard and ready once again, began to rock with orgasmic pleasure. The orgasm began slowly for her also, as if one false move and she'd lose it; then it became huge and uncontrollable. Liza was ramming her with the huge cock, and on the final thrust Hilary got in touch with the depth of her pain—and the ecstasy of her pleasure. Her groin filled with warmth while her ass felt too full—as if it would burst, as if she couldn't take any more. But she didn't flinch. She just took it all until the orgasmic rush became almost unbearable. It felt as if her whole body were coming and being ripped open at the same time.

Hilary cried out in a wail like an animal in pain, feeling a great release as she did. "Yes," she screamed in an untamed, uncontrolled, uninhibited howl. "Yesssssss."

EPILOGUE

Hilary opened the front door of the estate house. A young woman stood nervously waiting.

"Alizarin?"

"Yes," the young woman replied.

"Come in," Hilary instructed her.

Hilary led her to the morning room where Liza, her lover and mistress, awaited the newcomer.

The two looked Alizarin up and down, then glanced knowingly at one another. It was training time again.

You've heard of the writers
but didn't know where to find them

Samuel R. Delany • Pat Califia • Carol Queen • Lars Eighner • Felice Picano • Lucy Taylor • Aaron Travis • Michael Lassell • Red Jordan Arobateau • Michael Bronski • Tom Roche • Maxim Jakubowski • Michael Perkins • Camille Paglia • John Preston • Laura Antoniou • Alice Joanou • Cecilia Tan • Michael Perkins • Tuppy Owens • Trish Thomas • Lily Burana • Alison Tyler • Marco Vassi • Susie Bright • Randy Turoff • Allen Ellenzweig • Shar Rednour

You've seen the sexy images
but didn't know where to find them

Robert Chouraqui • Charles Gatewood • Richard Kern • Eric Kroll • Vivienne Maricevic • Housk Randall • Barbara Nitke • Trevor Watson • Mark Avers • Laura Graff • Michele Serchuk • Laurie Leber • John Willie • Sylvia Plachy • Romain Slocombe • Robert Mapplethorpe • Doris Kloster

You can find them all in
Masquerade

a publication designed expressly for the connoisseur of the erotic arts.

ORDER TODAY
SAVE 50%
1 year (6 issues) for $15; 2 years (12 issues) for only $25!

Essential. —*Skin Two*

The best newsletter I have ever seen! —*Secret International*

Very informative and enticing. —*Redemption*

A professional, insider's look at the world of erotica. —*Screw*

I recommend a subscription to **MASQUERADE**... It's good stuff. —*Black Sheets*

MASQUERADE presents some of the best articles on erotica, fetishes, sex clubs, the politics of porn and every conceivable issue of sex and sexuality. —*Factsheet Five*

Fabulous. —*Tuppy Owens*

MASQUERADE is absolutely lovely ... marvelous images. —*Le Boudoir Noir*

Highly recommended. —*Eidos*

DIRECT

Masquerade/Direct • DEPT BMMQC6 • 801 Second Avenue • New York, NY 10017 • FAX: 212.986.7355
MC/VISA orders can be placed by calling our toll-free number: 800.375.2356

☐ PLEASE SEND ME A 1 YEAR SUBSCRIPTION FOR $30 *NOW* $15 !
☐ PLEASE SEND ME A 2 YEAR SUBSCRIPTION FOR $60 *NOW* $25!

NAME _____
ADDRESS _____
CITY _____ STATE _____ ZIP _____
TEL (___) _____
PAYMENT: ☐ CHECK ☐ MONEY ORDER ☐ VISA ☐ MC
CARD # _____ EXP. DATE _____

No C.O.D. orders. Please make all checks payable to Masquerade/Direct. Payable in U.S. currency only.

MASQUERADE BOOKS

MASQUERADE

ATAULLAH MARDAAN
KAMA HOURI/DEVA DASI
$7.95/512-3
Two legendary tales of the East in one spectacular volume. *Kama Houri* details the life of a sheltered Western woman who finds herself living within the confines of a harem—where she discovers herself thrilled with the extent of her servitude. *Deva Dasi* is a tale dedicated to the cult of the Dasis—the sacred women of India who devoted their lives to the fulfillment of the senses—while revealing the sexual rites of Shiva.

"...memorable for the author's ability to evoke India present and past.... Mardaan excels in crowding her pages with the sights and smells of India, and her erotic descriptions are convincingly realistic."
—Michael Perkins,
The Secret Record: Modern Erotic Literature

J. P. KANSAS
ANDREA AT THE CENTER
$6.50/498-4
Kidnapped! Lithe and lovely young Andrea is whisked away to a distant retreat. Gradually, she is introduced to the ways of the Center, and soon becomes quite friendly with its other inhabitants—all of whom are learning to abandon restraint in their pursuit of the deepest sexual satisfaction. This tale of the ultimate sexual training facility is a nationally bestselling title and a classic of modern erotica.

VISCOUNT LADYWOOD
GYNECOCRACY
$9.95/511-5
An infamous story of female domination returns to print. Julian, whose parents feel he shows just a bit too much spunk, is sent to a very special private school, in hopes that he will learn to discipline his wayward soul. Once there, Julian discovers that his program of study has been devised by the deliciously stern Mademoiselle de Chambonnard. In no time, Julian is learning the many ways of pleasure—under the firm hand of this demanding headmistress.

CHARLOTTE ROSE, EDITOR
THE 50 BEST PLAYGIRL FANTASIES
$6.50/460-7
A steamy selection of women's fantasies straight from the pages of *Playgirl*—the leading magazine of sexy entertainment for women. These tales of seduction—specially selected by no less an authority than Charlotte Rose, author of such bestselling women's erotica as *Women at Work* and *The Doctor is In*—are sure to set your pulse racing. From the innocent to the insatiable, these women let no fantasy go unexplored.

N. T. MORLEY
THE PARLOR
$6.50/496-8
Lovely Kathryn gives in to the ultimate temptation. The mysterious John and Sarah ask her to be their slave—an idea that turns Kathryn on so much that she can't refuse! But who are these two mysterious strangers? Little by little, Kathryn not only learns to serve, but comes to know the inner secrets of her stunning keepers.

J. A. GUERRA, EDITOR
**COME QUICKLY:
FOR COUPLES ON THE GO**
$6.50/461-5
The increasing pace of daily life is no reason to forgo a little carnal pleasure whenever the mood strikes. Here are over sixty of the hottest fantasies around—all designed to get you going in less time than it takes to dial 976. A super-hot volume especially for couples on a modern schedule.

ERICA BRONTE
LUST, INC.
$6.50/467-4
Lust, Inc. explores the extremes of passion that lurk beneath even the coldest, most business-like exteriors. Join in the sexy escapades of a group of high-powered professionals whose idea of office decorum is like nothing you've ever encountered! Business attire not required....

VANESSA DURIÈS
THE TIES THAT BIND
$6.50/510-7
The incredible confessions of a thrillingly unconventional woman. From the first page, this chronicle of dominance and submission will keep you gasping with its vivid depictions of sensual abandon. At the hand of Masters Georges, Patrick, Pierre and others, this submissive seductress experiences pleasures she never knew existed....

M. S. VALENTINE
THE CAPTIVITY OF CELIA
$6.50/453-4
Colin is mistakenly considered the prime suspect in a murder, forcing him to seek refuge with his cousin, Sir Jason Hardwicke. In exchange for Colin's safety, Jason demands Celia's unquestioning submission—knowing she will do anything to protect her lover. Sexual extortion!

AMANDA WARE
BOUND TO THE PAST
$6.50/452-6
Anne accepts a research assignment in a Tudor mansion. Upon arriving, she finds herself aroused by James, a descendant of the mansion's owners. Together they uncover the perverse desires of the mansion's long-dead master—desires that bind Anne inexorably to the past—not to mention the bedpost!

BUY ANY 4 BOOKS & CHOOSE 1 ADDITIONAL BOOK, OF EQUAL OR LESSER VALUE, AS YOUR FREE GIFT

MASQUERADE BOOKS

SACHI MIZUNO
SHINJUKU NIGHTS
$6.50/493-3
Another tour through the lives and libidos of the seductive East, from the author of Passion in Tokyo. No one is better that Sachi Mizuno at weaving an intricate web of sensual desire, wherein many characters are ensnared and enraptured by the demands of their long-denied carnal natures. One by one, each surrenders social convention for the unashamed pleasures of the flesh.

PASSION IN TOKYO
$6.50/454-2
Tokyo—one of Asia's most historic and seductive cities. Come behind the closed doors of its citizens, and witness the many pleasures that await. Lusty men and women from every stratum of Japanese society free themselves of all inhibitions....

MARTINE GLOWINSKI
POINT OF VIEW
$6.50/433-X
With the assistance of her new, unexpectedly kinky lover, she discovers and explores her exhibitionist tendencies—until there is virtually nothing she won't do before the horny audiences her man arranges! Unabashed acting out for the sophisticated voyeur.

RICHARD McGOWAN
A HARLOT OF VENUS
$6.50/425-9
A highly fanciful, epic tale of lust on Mars! Cavortio—the most famous and sought-after courtesan in the cosmopolitan city of Venus—finds love and much more during her adventures with some of the most remarkable characters in recent erotic fiction.

M. ORLANDO
THE ARCHITECTURE OF DESIRE
Introduction by Richard Manton.
$6.50/490-9
Two novels in one special volume! In *The Hotel Justine*, an elite clientele is afforded the opportunity to have any and all desires satisfied. *The Villa Sin* is inherited by a beautiful woman who soon realizes that the legacy of the ancestral estate includes bizarre erotic ceremonies. Two pieces of prime real estate.

CHET ROTHWELL
KISS ME, KATHERINE
$5.95/410-0
Beautiful Katherine can hardly believe her luck. Not only is she married to the charming and oh-so-agreeable Nelson, she's free to live out all her erotic fantasies with other men. Katherine has discovered Nelson to be far more devoted than the average spouse—and the duo soon begin exploring a relationship more demanding than marriage! Soon, Katherine's desires become more than any one man can handle.

MARCO VASSI
THE STONED APOCALYPSE
$5.95/401-1/mass market
"Marco Vassi is our champion sexual energist."—*VLS*
During his lifetime, Marco Vassi praised by writers as diverse as Gore Vidal and Norman Mailer, and his reputation was worldwide. *The Stoned Apocalypse* is Vassi's autobiography; chronicling a cross-country trip on America's erotic byways, it offers a rare glimpse of a generation's sexual imagination.

ROBIN WILDE
TABITHA'S TICKLE
$6.50/468-2
Tabitha's back! The story of this vicious vixen—and her torturously tantalizing cohorts—didn't end with *Tabitha's Tease*. Once again, men fall under the spell of scrumptious co-eds and find themselves enslaved to demands and desires they never dreamed existed. Think it's a man's world? Guess again. With Tabitha around, no man gets what he wants until she's completely satisfied—and, maybe, not even then....

TABITHA'S TEASE
$5.95/387-2
When poor Robin arrives at The Valentine Academy, he finds himself subject to the torturous teasing of Tabitha—the Academy's most notoriously domineering co-ed. But Tabitha is pledge-mistress of a secret sorority dedicated to enslaving young men. Robin finds himself the utterly helpless (and wildly excited) captive of Tabitha & Company's weird desires! A marathon of ticklish torture!

ERICA BRONTE
PIRATE'S SLAVE
$5.95/376-7
Lovely young Erica is stranded in a country where lust knows no bounds. Desperate to escape, she finds herself trading her firm, luscious body to any and all men willing and able to help her. Her adventure has its ups and downs, ins and outs—all to the undeniable pleasure of lusty Erica!

CHARLES G. WOOD
HELLFIRE
$5.95/358-9
A vicious murderer is running amok in New York's sexual underground—and Nick O'Shay, a virile detective with the NYPD, plunges deep into the case. He soon becomes embroiled in an elusive world of fleshly extremes, hunting a madman seeking to purge America with fire and blood sacrifices. Set in New York's infamous sexual underground.

CLAIRE BAEDER, EDITOR
LA DOMME: A DOMINATRIX ANTHOLOGY
$5.95/366-X
A steamy smorgasbord of female domination! Erotic literature has long been filled with heartstopping portraits of domineering women, and now the most memorable have been brought together in one beautifully brutal volume. A must for all fans of true Woman Power.

MASQUERADE BOOKS

CHARISSE VAN DER LYN
SEX ON THE NET
$5.95/399-6
Electrifying erotica from one of the Internet's hottest and most widely read authors. Encounters of all kinds—straight, lesbian, dominant/submissive and all sorts of extreme passions—are explored in thrilling detail.

STANLEY CARTEN
NAUGHTY MESSAGE
$5.95/333-3
Wesley Arthur discovers a lascivious message on his answering machine. Aroused beyond his wildest dreams by the acts described, Wesley becomes obsessed with tracking down the woman behind the seductive voice. His search takes him through strip clubs, sex parlors and no-tell motels—and finally to his randy reward....

AKBAR DEL PIOMBO
DUKE COSIMO
$4.95/3052-0
A kinky romp played out against the boudoirs, bathrooms and ballrooms of the European nobility, who seem to do nothing all day except each other. The lifestyles of the rich and licentious are revealed in all their glory.

A CRUMBLING FAÇADE
$4.95/3043-1
The return of that incorrigible rogue, Henry Pike, who continues his pursuit of sex, fair or otherwise, in the most elegant homes of the most debauched aristocrats.

CAROLE REMY
FANTASY IMPROMPTU
$6.50/513-1
A mystical, musical journey into the deepest recesses of a woman's soul. Kidnapped and held in a remote island retreat, Chantal—a renowned erotic writer—finds herself catering to every sexual whim of the mysterious and arousing Bran. Bran is determined to bring Chantal to a full embracing of her sensual nature, even while revealing himself to be something far more than human....

BEAUTY OF THE BEAST
$5.95/332-5
A shocking tell-all, written from the point-of-view of a prize-winning reporter. And what reporting she does! All the secrets of an uninhibited life are revealed, and each lusty tableau is painted in glowing colors.

DAVID AARON CLARK
THE MARQUIS DE SADE'S JULIETTE
$4.95/240-X
The Marquis de Sade's infamous Juliette returns—and emerges as the most perverse and destructive nightstalker modern New York will ever know. One by one, the innocent are drawn in by Juliette's empty promise of immortality, only to fall prey to her strange and deadly lusts.

ANONYMOUS
NADIA
$5.95/267-1
Follow the delicious but neglected Nadia as she works to wring every drop of pleasure out of life—despite an unhappy marriage. A classic title providing a peek into the secret sexual lives of another time and place.

NIGEL McPARR
THE STORY OF A VICTORIAN MAID
$5.95/241-8
What were the Victorians really like? Chances are, no one believes they were as stuffy as their Queen, but who would have imagined such unbridled libertines!

TITIAN BERESFORD
CINDERELLA
$6.50/500-X
Beresford triumphs again with this intoxicating tale, filled with castle dungeons and tightly corseted ladies-in-waiting, naughty viscounts and impossibly cruel masturbatrixes—nearly every conceivable method of erotic torture is explored and described in lush, vivid detail.

JUDITH BOSTON
$6.50/525-5
Young Edward would have been lucky to get the stodgy old companion he thought his parents had hired for him. Instead, an exquisite woman arrives at his door, and Edward finds his lewd behavior never goes unpunished by the unflinchingly severe Judith Boston! Together they take the downward path to perversion!

NINA FOXTON
$5.95/443-7
An aristocrat finds herself bored by run-of-the-mill amusements for "ladies of good breeding." Instead of taking tea with proper gentlemen, naughty Nina "milks" them of their most private essences. No man ever says "No" to Nina!

P. N. DEDEAUX
THE NOTHING THINGS
$5.95/404-6
Beta Beta Rho—highly exclusive and widely honored—has taken on a new group of pledges. The five women will be put through the most grueling of ordeals, and punished severely for any shortcomings—much to everyone's delight!

LYN DAVENPORT
THE GUARDIAN II
$6.50/505-0
The tale of Felicia Brookes—the lovely young woman held in submission by the demanding Sir Rodney Wentworth—continues in this volume of sensual surprises. No sooner has Felicia come to love Rodney than she discovers that she must now accustom herself to the guardianship of the debauched Duke of Smithton. How long will this last? Surely Rodney will rescue her from the domination of this stranger. Won't he?

BUY ANY 4 BOOKS & CHOOSE 1 ADDITIONAL BOOK, OF EQUAL OR LESSER VALUE, AS YOUR FREE GIFT

MASQUERADE BOOKS

DOVER ISLAND
$5.95/384-8
Dr. David Kelly has planted the seeds of his dream—a Corporal Punishment Resort. Soon, many people from varied walks of life descend upon this isolated retreat, intent on fulfilling their every desire. Including Marcy Harris, the perfect partner for the lustful Doctor....

THE GUARDIAN
$5.95/371-6
Felicia grew up under the tutelage of the lash—and she learned her lessons well. Sir Rodney Wentworth has long searched for a woman capable of fulfilling his cruel desires, and after learning of Felicia's talents, sends for her. Felicia discovers that the "position" offered her is delightfully different than anything she could have expected!

LIZBETH DUSSEAU
THE APPLICANT
$6.50/501-8
"Adventuresome young women who enjoys being submissive sought by married couple in early forties. Expect no limits." Hilary answers an ad, hoping to find someone who can meet her special needs. The beautiful Liza turns out to be a flawless mistress, and together with her husband, Oliver, she trains Hilary to be the perfect servant. Scandalous sexual servitude.

ANTHONY BOBARZYNSKI
STASI SLUT
$4.95/3050-4
Adina lives in East Germany, where she can only dream about the freedoms of the West. But then she meets a group of ruthless and corrupt STASI agents. They use her body for their own perverse gratification, while she opts to use her talents and attractions in a final bid for total freedom!

JOCELYN JOYCE
PRIVATE LIVES
$4.95/309-0
The lecherous habits of the illustrious make for a sizzling tale of French erotic life. A widow has a craving for a young busboy; he's sleeping with a rich businessman's wife; her husband is minding his sex business elsewhere! Scandalous sexual entanglements run throughout this tale of upper crust lust!

SARAH JACKSON
SANCTUARY
$5.95/318-X
Sanctuary explores both the unspeakable debauchery of court life and the unimaginable privations of monastic solitude, leading the voracious and the virtuous on a collision course that brings history to throbbing life.

THE WILD HEART
$4.95/3007-5
A luxury hotel is the setting for this artful web of sex, desire, and love. A newlywed sees sex as a duty, while her hungry husband tries to awaken her to its tender joys. A Parisian entertains wealthy guests for the love of money. Each episode provides a new variation in this lusty Grand Hotel!

LOUISE BELHAVEL
FRAGRANT ABUSES
$4.95/88-2
The saga of Clara and Iris continues as the now-experienced girls enjoy themselves with a new circle of worldly friends whose imaginations match their own. Perversity follows the lusty ladies around the globe!

SARA H. FRENCH
MASTER OF TIMBERLAND
$5.95/327-9
A tale of sexual slavery at the ultimate paradise resort. One of our bestselling titles, this trek to Timberland has ignited passions the world over—and stands poised to become one of modern erotica's legendary tales.

MARY LOVE
MASTERING MARY SUE
$5.95/351-1
Mary Sue is a rich nymphomaniac whose husband is determined to declare her mentally incompetent and gain control of her fortune. He brings her to a castle where, to Mary Sue's delight, she is unleashed for a veritable sex-fest!

THE BEST OF MARY LOVE
$4.95/3099-7
Mary Love leaves no coupling untried and no extreme unexplored in these scandalous selections from *Mastering Mary Sue*, *Ecstasy on Fire*, *Vice Park Place*, *Wanda*, and *Naughtier at Night*.

AMARANTHA KNIGHT
THE DARKER PASSIONS: THE PICTURE OF DORIAN GRAY
$6.50/342-2
Amarantha Knight takes on Oscar Wilde, resulting in a fabulously decadent tale of highly personal changes. One young man finds his most secret desires laid bare by a portrait far more revealing than he could have imagined....

THE DARKER PASSIONS READER
$6.50/432-1
The best moments from Knight's phenomenally popular Darker Passions series. Here are the most eerily erotic passages from her acclaimed sexual reworkings of *Dracula*, *Frankenstein*, *Dr. Jekyll & Mr. Hyde* and *The Fall of the House of Usher*.

THE DARKER PASSIONS: THE FALL OF THE HOUSE OF USHER
$6.50/528-X
The Master and Mistress of the house of Usher indulge in every form of decadence, and initiate their guests into the many pleasures to be found in utter submission.

THE DARKER PASSIONS: DR. JEKYLL AND MR. HYDE
$4.95/227-2
It is a story of incredible transformations achieved through mysterious experiments. Explore the steamy possibilities of a tale where no one is quite who—or what—they seem. Victorian bedrooms explode with hidden demons!

MASQUERADE BOOKS

THE DARKER PASSIONS: FRANKENSTEIN
$5.95/248-5
What if you could create a living human? What shocking acts could it be taught to perform, to desire? Find out what pleasures await those who play God....

THE DARKER PASSIONS: DRACULA
$5.95/326-0
The infamous erotic retelling of the Vampire legend. "Well-written and imaginative, Amarantha Knight gives fresh impetus to this myth, taking us through the sexual and sadistic scenes with details that keep us reading.... A classic in itself has been added to the shelves." —*Divinity*

PAUL LITTLE

THE BEST OF PAUL LITTLE
$6.50/469-0
One of Masquerade's all-time best-selling authors. Known throughout the world for his fantastic portrayals of punishment and pleasure, Little never fails to push readers over the edge of sensual excitement.

ALL THE WAY
$6.95/509-3
Two excruciating novels from Paul Little in one hot volume! *Going All the Way* features an unhappy man who tries to purge himself of the memory of his lover with a series of quirky and uninhibited lovers. *Pushover* tells the story of a serial spanker and his celebrated exploits.

THE DISCIPLINE OF ODETTE
$5.95/334-1
Odette's was sure marriage would rescue her from her family's "corrections." To her horror, she discovers that her beloved has also been raised on discipline. A shocking erotic coupling!

THE PRISONER
$5.95/330-9
Judge Black has built a secret room below a penitentiary, where he sentences the prisoners to hours of exhibition and torment while his friends watch. Judge Black's House of Corrections is equipped with one purpose in mind: to administer his own brand of rough justice!

TEARS OF THE INQUISITION
$4.95/146-2
The incomparable Paul Little delivers a staggering account of pleasure and punishment. "There was a tickling inside her as her nervous system reminded her she was ready for sex. But before her was...the Inquisitor!" One of history's most infamous periods comes to throbbing life via the perverse imagination of Paul Little.

DOUBLE NOVEL
$4.95/86-0
The Metamorphosis of Lisette Joyaux tells the story of a young woman initiated into a new and incredible world of lesbian lusts. *The Story of Monique* reveals the twisted sexual rituals that beckon the ripe and willing Monique.

CHINESE JUSTICE AND OTHER STORIES
$4.95/153-5
The story of the excruciating pleasures and delicious punishments inflicted on foreigners under the leaders of the Boxer Rebellion. Each foreign woman is brought before the authorities and grilled, much to the delight of their perverse captors. Scandalous deeds and shocking exploitation!

CAPTIVE MAIDENS
$5.95/440-2
Three beautiful young women find themselves powerless against the debauched landowners of 1824 England. They are banished to a sexual slave colony, and corrupted by every imaginable perversion. Soon, they come to crave the treatment of their unrelenting captors.

SLAVE ISLAND
$5.95/441-0
A leisure cruise is waylaid by Lord Henry Philbrock, a sadistic genius. The ship's passengers are kidnapped and spirited to his island prison, where the women are trained to accommodate the most bizarre sexual cravings of the rich, the famous, the pampered and the perverted.

ALIZARIN LAKE

SEX ON DOCTOR'S ORDERS
$5.95/402-X
Beth, a nubile young nurse, uses her considerable skills to further medical science by offering incomparable and insatiable assistance in the gathering of important specimens. Soon, an assortment of randy characters is lending a hand in this highly erotic work. No man leaves naughty Nurse Beth's station without surrendering what she needs!

THE EROTIC ADVENTURES OF HARRY TEMPLE
$4.95/127-6
Harry Temple's memoirs chronicle his amorous adventures from his initiation at the hands of insatiable sirens, through his stay at a house of hot repute, to his encounters with a chastity-belted nympho!

JOHN NORMAN

TARNSMAN OF GOR
$6.95/486-0
This controversial series returns! *Tarnsman* finds Tarl Cabot transported to Counter-Earth, better known as Gor. He must quickly accustom himself to the ways of this world, including the caste system which exalts some as Priest-Kings or Warriors, and debases others as slaves. A spectacular world unfolds in this first volume of John Norman's Gorean series.

OUTLAW OF GOR
$6.95/487-9
In this second volume, Tarl Cabot returns to Gor, where he might reclaim both his woman and his role of Warrior. But upon arriving, he discovers that his name, his city and the names of those he loves have become unspeakable. Cabot has become an outlaw, and must discover his new purpose on this strange planet, where danger stalks the outcast, and even simple answers have their price....

BUY ANY 4 BOOKS & CHOOSE 1 ADDITIONAL BOOK, OF EQUAL OR LESSER VALUE, AS YOUR FREE GIFT

MASQUERADE BOOKS

PRIEST-KINGS OF GOR
$6.95/488-7
The third volume of John Norman's million-selling Gor series. Tarl Cabot searches for the truth about his lovely wife Talena. Does she live, or was she destroyed by the mysterious, all-powerful Priest-Kings? Cabot is determined to find out—even while knowing that no one who has approached the mountain stronghold of the Priest-Kings has ever returned alive....

NOMADS OF GOR
$6.95/527-1
Another provocative trip to the barbaric and mysterious world of Gor. Norman's heroic Tarnsman finds his way across this Counter-Earth, pledged to serve the Priest-Kings in their quest for survival. Unfortunately for Cabot, his mission leads him to the savage Wagon People—nomads who may very well kill before surrendering any secrets....

RACHEL PEREZ
AFFINITIES
$4.95/113-6
"Kelsy had a liking for cool upper-class blondes, the long-legged girls from Lake Forest and Winnetka who came into the city to cruise the lesbian bars on Halsted, looking for breathless ecstasies...." A scorching tale of lesbian libidos unleashed, from a writer more than capable of exploring every nuance of female passion in vivid detail.

SYDNEY ST. JAMES
RIVE GAUCHE
$5.95/317-1
The Latin Quarter, Paris, circa 1920. Expatriate bohemians couple with abandon—before eventually abandoning their ambitions amidst the intoxicating temptations waiting to be indulged in every bedroom.

GARDEN OF DELIGHT
$4.95/3058-X
A vivid account of sexual awakening that follows an innocent but insatiably curious young woman's journey from the furtive, forbidden joys of dormitory life to the unabashed carnality of the wild world.

DON WINSLOW
PRIVATE PLEASURES
$6.50/504-2
An assortment of sensual encounters designed to appeal to the most discerning reader. Frantic voyeurs, licentious exhibitionists, and everyday lovers are here displayed in all their wanton glory—proving again that fleshly pleasures have no more apt chronicler than Don Winslow.

THE INSATIABLE MISTRESS OF ROSEDALE
$6.50/494-1
The story of the perfect couple: Edward and Lady Penelope, who reside in beautiful and mysterious Rosedale manor. While Edward is a true connoisseur of sexual perversion, it is Lady Penelope whose mastery of complete sensual pleasure makes their home infamous. Indulging one another's bizarre whims is a way of life for this wicked couple, and none who encounter the extravagances of Rosedale will forget what they've learned....

SECRETS OF CHEATEM MANOR
$6.50/434-8
Edward returns to his late father's estate, to find it being run by the majestic Lady Amanda. Edward can hardly believe his luck—Lady Amanda is assisted by her two beautiful, lonely daughters, Catherine and Prudence. What the randy young man soon comes to realize is the love of discipline that all three beauties share.

KATERINA IN CHARGE
$5.95/409-7
When invited to a country retreat by a mysterious couple, two randy young ladies can hardly resist! But do they have any idea what they're in for? Whatever the case, the imperious Katerina will make her desires known very soon—and demand that they be fulfilled... Sexual innocence subjugated and defiled.

THE MANY PLEASURES OF IRONWOOD
$5.95/310-4
Seven lovely young women are employed by The Ironwood Sportsmen's Club, where their natural talents are put to creative use. A small and exclusive club with seven carefully selected sexual connoisseurs, Ironwood is dedicated to the relentless pursuit of sensual pleasure.

CLAIRE'S GIRLS
$5.95/442-9
You knew when she walked by that she was something special. She was one of Claire's girls, a woman carefully dressed and groomed to fill a role, to capture a look, to fit an image crafted by the sophisticated proprietress of an exclusive escort agency. High-class whores blow the roof off in this blow-by-blow account of life behind the closed doors of a sophisticated brothel.

N. WHALLEN
TAU'TEVU
$6.50/426-7
In a mysterious land, the statuesque and beautiful Vivian learns to subject herself to the hand of a mysterious man. He systematically helps her prove her own strength, and brings to life in her an unimagined sensual fire. But who is this man, who goes only by the name of Orpheo?

COMPLIANCE
$5.95/356-2
Fourteen stories exploring the pleasures of ultimate release. Characters from all walks of life learn to trust in the skills of others, hoping to experience the thrilling liberation of sexual submission. Here are the many joys to be found in some of the most forbidden sexual practices around....

THE CLASSIC COLLECTION
PROTESTS, PLEASURES, RAPTURES
$5.95/400-3
Invited for an allegedly quiet weekend at a country vicarage, a young woman is stunned to find herself surrounded by shocking acts of sexual sadism. Soon, her curiosity is piqued, and she begins to explore her own capacities for cruelty. The ultimate tale of an extraordinary woman's erotic awakening.

MASQUERADE BOOKS

THE YELLOW ROOM
$5.95/378-3
The "yellow room" holds the secrets of lust, lechery, and the lash. There, bare-bottomed, spread-eagled, and open to the world, demure Alice Darvell soon learns to love her lickings. In the second tale, hot heiress Rosa Coote and her lusty servants whip up numerous adventures in punishment and pleasure.

SCHOOL DAYS IN PARIS
$5.95/325-2
The rapturous chronicles of a well-spent youth! Few Universities provide the profound and pleasurable lessons one learns in after-hours study—particularly if one is young and available, and lucky enough to have Paris as a playground. A stimulating look at the pursuits of young adulthood, set in a glittering city notorious for its amorous excesses.

MAN WITH A MAID
$4.95/307-4
The adventures of Jack and Alice have delighted readers for eight decades! A classic of its genre, *Man with a Maid* tells an outrageous tale of desire, revenge, and submission. This tale qualifies as one of the world's most popular adult novels—with over 200,000 copies in print!

CONFESSIONS OF A CONCUBINE III: PLEASURE'S PRISONER
$5.95/357-0
Filled with pulse-pounding excitement—including a daring escape from the harem and an encounter with an unspeakable sadist—*Pleasure's Prisoner* adds an unforgettable chapter to this thrilling confessional.

CLASSIC EROTIC BIOGRAPHIES

JENNIFER
$4.95/107-1
The return of one of the Sexual Revolution's most notorious heroines. From the bedroom of a notoriously insatiable dancer to an uninhibited ashram, *Jennifer* traces the exploits of one thoroughly modern woman as she lustfully explores the limits of her own sexuality.

JENNIFER III
$5.95/292-2
The further adventures of erotica's most daring heroine. Jennifer, the quintessential beautiful blonde, has a photographer's eye for details—particularly of the masculine variety! One by one, her subjects submit to her demands for sensual pleasure, becoming part of her now-infamous gallery of erotic conquests.

RHINOCEROS

KATHLEEN K.

SWEET TALKERS
$6.95/516-6
Kathleen K. ran a phone-sex company in the late 80s, and she opens up her diary for a very thought provoking peek at the life of a phone-sex operator—and reveals a number of secrets and surprises. Transcripts of actual conversations are included.

"If you enjoy eavesdropping on explicit conversations about sex... this book is for you." —Spectator

"Highly recommended." —Shiny International
Trade /$12.95/192-6

THOMAS S. ROCHE

DARK MATTER
$6.95/484-4
"*Dark Matter* is sure to please gender outlaws, body-mod junkies, goth vampires, boys who wish they were dykes, and anybody who's not to sure where the fine line should be drawn between pleasure and pain. It's a handful." —Pat Califia

"Here is the erotica of the cumming millenium: velvet-voiced but razor-tongued, tarted-up, but smart as a whip behind that smudged black eyeliner—encompassing every conceivable gender and several in between. You will be deliciously disturbed, but never disappointed." —Poppy Z. Brite

NOIROTICA: AN ANTHOLOGY OF EROTIC CRIME STORIES
$6.95/390-2
A collection of darkly sexy tales, taking place at the crossroads of the crime and erotic genres. Thomas S. Roche has gathered together some of today's finest writers of sexual fiction, all of whom explore the murky terrain where desire runs irrevocably afoul of the law.

ROMY ROSEN

SPUNK
$6.95/492-5
A tale of unearthly beauty, outrageous decadence, and brutal exploitation. Casey, a lovely model poised upon the verge of super-celebrity, falls for an insatiable young rock singer—not suspecting that his sexual appetite has led him to experiment with a dangerous new aphrodisiac. Casey becomes an addict, and her craving plunges her into a strange underworld, where bizarre sexual compulsions are indulged behind the most exclusive doors and the only chance for redemption lies with a shadowy young man with a secret of his own.

BUY ANY 4 BOOKS & CHOOSE 1 ADDITIONAL BOOK, OF EQUAL OR LESSER VALUE, AS YOUR FREE GIFT

MASQUERADE BOOKS

MOLLY WEATHERFIELD
CARRIE'S STORY
$6.95/485-2
"I had been Jonathan's slave for about a year when he told me he wanted to sell me at an auction. I wasn't in any condition to respond when he told me this…" Desire and depravity run rampant in this story of uncompromising mastery and irrevocable submission. A unique piece of erotica that is both thoughtful and hot!

"I was stunned by how well it was written and how intensely foreign I found its sexual world…. And, since this is a world I don't frequent… I thoroughly enjoyed the National Geo tour." —bOING bOING

"Hilarious and harrowing… just when you think things can't get any wilder, they do." —Black Sheets

CYBERSEX CONSORTIUM
CYBERSEX: THE PERV'S GUIDE TO FINDING SEX ON THE INTERNET
$6.95/471-2
You've heard the objections: cyberspace is soaked with sex. Okay—so where is it!? Tracking down the good stuff—the real good stuff—can waste an awful lot of expensive time, and frequently leave you high and dry. The Cybersex Consortium presents an easy-to-use guide for those intrepid adults who know what they want. No horny hacker can afford to pass up this map to the kinkiest rest stops on the Info Superhighway.

AMELIA G, EDITOR
BACKSTAGE PASSES
$6.95/438-0
Amelia G, editor of the goth-sex journal *Blue Blood*, has brought together some of today's most irreverent writers, each of whom has outdone themselves with an edgy, antic tale of modern lust. Punks, metalheads, and grunge-trash roam the pages of *Backstage Passes*, and no one knows their ways better…

GERI NETTICK WITH BETH ELLIOT
MIRRORS: PORTRAIT OF A LESBIAN TRANSSEXUAL
$6.95/435-6
The alternately heartbreaking and empowering story of one woman's long road to full selfhood. Born a male, Geri Nettick knew something just didn't fit. And even after coming to terms with her own gender dysphoria—and taking steps to correct it—she still fought to be accepted by the lesbian feminist community to which she felt she belonged. A fascinating, true tale of struggle and discovery.

DAVID MELTZER
UNDER
$6.95/290-6
The story of a 21st century sex professional living at the bottom of the social heap. After surgeries designed to increase his physical allure, corrupt government forces drive the cyber-gigolo underground—where even more bizarre cultures await him.

ORF
$6.95/110-1
He is the ultimate musician-hero—the idol of thousands, the fevered dream of many more. And like many musicians before him, he is misunderstood, misused—and totally out of control. Every last drop of feeling is squeezed from a modern-day troubadour and his lady love.

LAURA ANTONIOU, EDITOR
NO OTHER TRIBUTE
$6.95/294-9
A collection sure to challenge Political Correctness in a way few have before, with tales of women kept in bondage to their lovers by their deepest passions. Love pushes these women beyond acceptable limits, rendering them helpless to deny anything to the men and women they adore. A volume dedicated to all Slaves of Desire.

SOME WOMEN
$6.95/300-7
Over forty essays written by women actively involved in consensual dominance and submission. Professional mistresses, lifestyle leatherdykes, whipmakers, titleholders—women from every conceivable walk of life lay bare their true feelings about explosive issues.

BY HER SUBDUED
$6.95/281-7
These tales all involve women in control—of their lives, their loves, their men. So much in control that they can remorselessly break rules to become powerful goddesses of the men who sacrifice all to worship at their feet.

TRISTAN TAORMINO & DAVID AARON CLARK, EDITORS
RITUAL SEX
$6.95/391-0
While many people believe the body and soul to occupy almost completely independent realms, the many contributors to *Ritual Sex* know—and demonstrate—that the two share more common ground than society feels comfortable acknowledging. From personal memoirs of ecstatic revelation, to fictional quests to reconcile sex and spirit, *Ritual Sex* provides an unprecedented look at private life.

TAMMY JO ECKHART
PUNISHMENT FOR THE CRIME
$6.95/427-5
Peopled by characters of rare depth, these stories explore the true meaning of dominance and submission. From an encounter between two of society's most despised individuals, to the explorations of longtime friends, these tales take you where few others have ever dared….

AMARANTHA KNIGHT, EDITOR
SEDUCTIVE SPECTRES
$6.95/464-X
Breathtaking tours through the erotic supernatural via the macabre imaginations of today's best writers. Never before have ghostly encounters been so alluring, thanks to a cast of otherworldly characters well-acquainted with the pleasures of the flesh.

ORDERING IS EASY

MC/VISA orders can be placed by calling our toll-free number
PHONE 800-375-2356/FAX 212-986-7355/E-MAIL masqbks@aol.com
or mail this coupon to:
MASQUERADE DIRECT
DEPT. BMMQC6 801 2ND AVE., NY, NY 10017

BUY ANY FOUR BOOKS AND CHOOSE ONE ADDITIONAL BOOK, OF EQUAL OR LESSER VALUE, AS YOUR FREE GIFT.

QTY.	TITLE	NO.	PRICE
			FREE
			FREE

We Never Sell, Give or Trade Any Customer's Name.

SUBTOTAL
POSTAGE and HANDLING
TOTAL

In the U.S., please add $1.50 for the first book and 75¢ for each additional book; in Canada, add $2.00 for the first book and $1.25 for each additional book. Foreign countries: add $4.00 for the first book and $2.00 for each additional book. No C.O.D. orders. Please make all checks payable to Masquerade Books. Payable in U.S. currency only. New York state residents add 8.25% sales tax. Please allow 4-6 weeks for delivery.

NAME_____

ADDRESS_____

CITY_____ STATE_____ ZIP_____

TEL( )_____

E-MAIL_____

PAYMENT: ☐ CHECK   ☐ MONEY ORDER   ☐ VISA   ☐ MC

CARD NO_____ EXP. DATE_____